MW01135556

SHE WORE THE NAME

THERESA A. WARD

She Wore The Name
Copyright © 2021 by Theresa A. Ward

All rights reserved. No part of this publication may be
reproduced, distributed, or transmitted in any form or
by any means, including photocopying, recording, or
other electronic or mechanical methods, without the prior
written permission of the author, except in the case of
brief quotations embodied in critical reviews and certain
other non-commercial uses permitted by copyright law.

Tellwell Talent
www.tellwell.ca

ISBN
978-0-2288-5444-9 (Hardcover)
978-0-2288-5443-2 (Paperback)
978-0-2288-5445-6 (eBook)

HOW THE NAME OF
THE BOOK CAME INTO FRUITION

This book started off as a novella. The year, 2015, in a suburb of Atlanta, Georgia. Three other women and I got together in the home of one of the writers. Each woman had to come up with an idea for the name of our collaboration. I penned the name, "She Wore The Name." It was chosen out of the other names submitted, to be used as the title.

Life happened after we started the book. Years passed, and each writer went their own way with their respective manuscripts. I relocated back to my hometown of Kansas City, MO, but not one day went by in my heart without thinking about getting my story published. Winds calmed down after several years and a door opened for me to take a leap of faith to become published.

She Wore The Name is a salute to every woman on their journey to be that woman who wears her name extraordinarily.

Thank you for being the wind under my feet.

Women just inspire each other in that way.

A testimony, a smile, a phone call, a hug, a laugh, and/or a word of encouragement can keep you in place, steady, ready, and pushing until your destiny comes.

That's how amazing we are as women.

Salute to the best!

Thank you for being who you are in your name!\

Theresa Ward
Author of She Wore The Name

THANK YOU

*I personally want to invite
you to turn a page with me.*

Whether you are a first-time reader or a progressive reader,
I want to directly thank you for purchasing *She Wore The Name.*
You will not be disappointed as you read through a succession of
Fear, Love, Disappointment, Whodunit, and Suspense!
It is a book you will not want to put down
or share with another reader!
Your purchase allows me to continue to
write and the ability to give back.
Every purchase means that much Not returning it, pays
it forward for much-needed work in our communities.
Please purchase a cup of coffee, tea, or a glass
of wine or champagne on me personally!

My book was budgeted at a lower cost point
than other books of my genre, so I could "wage
it forward" to all my marvelous readers!

So, sashay your way to the local coffee
shop or winery as my gift to you!

You're valued as wearing your name well!

Thank you for your investment in me!

RECOGNITION

To those who attended Southeast High School of Kansas City, MO,

To those who have and are attending Penn Valley Community College,

or one of the other Greater Metropolitan Colleges of Kansas City, MO,

To those who have and are attending the prestigious Tuskegee University of Tuskegee Alabama

Or our sister school, Hampton University:

I consider it an honor to have attended or to have been affiliated with these amazing institutions of learning.

Salute to you all!

You are the most excellent!

MY MARKERS AND GAUGES

I would like to give tribute and much reverence to the following women for being inspirations for me.

I have held on to your skirt-tails for direction and encouragement throughout my journey.

Thank you

Mrs. Michelle Obama
First Lady Melania Trump
Oprah Winfrey
Condoleezza Rice
Susan Taylor
Harris Faulkner
The late Nina Simone
Iyanla Vanzant
Ms. Patti Labelle
Whoopi Goldberg
Ms. Wendy Williams
Mo'Nique
Serena Williams
Dana Owens *(Queen Latifah)*
Remy Ma
Tammy Rivera *(The better half of Waka Flocka)*, smile
Da-Brat

At hand, there are many men that I admire. There is not enough room to acknowledge them all.

Much respect and admiration to them all!

Two, though, I would like to acknowledge:

President Barack Hussein Obama

Patrick Mahomes, for leading the Kansas City Chiefs to "Two Super Bowls."

AN INVITATION

My book captures the trials, tribulations, and experiences of just one. Her name happens to be Sarai Chameleon. The choices you make, and the outcome of those decisions, could possibly be linked to your extraordinary name as well. How you manage that name and then use it, for failure or success, is up to you. The struggles of power and challenges of every woman should be shared. That is why I think my book should be on your bookshelf.

MY MISSIVE

I have decided to challenge myself to challenge me every
day: I will look in the mirror till I cry or laugh. In me,
there is humor, charm, and popularity, but there is also,
on the far end, despair. I have chosen not to let the
Dark-Man take me. The sun rising every day tells me
I have a new chance at life, and I can get it right.
So, if I want to run in the rain with no clothing on or
shave my hair off and wear red lipstick with my fair
skin, I will do just that. If it means me pleasing myself
and the orgasm belongs to me exclusively, it shall be.
A tattoo with my conservatism is my business, and by the
way, my tattoo says "forget you" on my behind. If I must
change my name to Miss Blue and move to the other side
of the world to have peace and no one see me again, then
that is my defining moment, and no one can have it.
I am happy with this one life given to me. I am
beautiful, fabulous, needed, and loved.
I am a harvester of souls, and I am working to be
the best I can with the name given to me.

My name is Theresa Ward, and this is how I wear my name.

MY FAVORITE QUOTE

I do not like the woman who squanders life for fame.
Give me the woman who, living, makes a name
Martial

DEDICATIONS

This book is dedicated to "You"
The Soldier
The Woman who went back to school to get her degree
The Single Mother
The Grandmother
The Daughter who is taking care of a parent
The Woman in corporate who helped a sister get a job
The Woman who escaped an abusive relationship
The Woman who survived cancer—You ROCK!
The Woman who decided to step out and fulfill her dreams
The Bus Driver
The Artist
The Little Woman
The Full-Figured Woman
The Hallelujah-here-is-Jesus Woman!
The Undecided Woman
The Handicapped Woman
The Weave Wearer, Afro Queen, Natural and Permed Woman
The Vegan
And, of course, Women of all Nationalities!

This book was written by me for you
I believe you are someone "Famous"
And you wear your name "Flawlessly"

Enjoy the read

TABLE OF CONTENTS

"It is not the going out of port but the coming in that determines the success of the voyage." Henry Beecher Ward

"I do not like the woman who squanders life for fame. Give me the woman who, living, makes a name." Martial

CHAPTER I

THORNS AND THISTLES

*"Difficulties show men what they are. In case of
difficulty, remember that God has pitted you against
a tough antagonist that you may be a conqueror,
and this cannot be without toil."*
Epictetus

Sarai begins to dream that her desolate womb cries out loudly, void like a hollow drum, echoing beats of anguish and begging for atonement with every groan. The roaring thunder of her past and the soft sweet whisper of her future clash just over the horizon of her tattered soul. The sounds of the confrontation can't be ignored. Sarai lays down the past at the foot of her future. She stands poised with arms open, welcoming her new beginning.

Sarai Chameleon is the younger of two African American sisters. She was born with the proverbial golden spoon in her mouth and drinking from the silver cup of generational redbone wealth. Her family power and influence spans from the borders of Montgomery, Alabama, to the panhandle of Pensacola, Florida, on across Cairo, Georgia, to the Savannah coastline, down past the Louisiana Bijous, and over miles of the Atlantic Ocean to the tip of Portugal.

She was born of the seed of Black slave owners, traders, builders, and inventors. Sarai has it all, yet she has nothing. Her life is empty and nomadic, spinning out of control with every twist and turn. Her destiny shackled, tangled by the invasion of growing thorns and thistles. Her mind is clouded by rotting straw and hay. Her money and family connections bring no relief from the cesspool of fear and doubt that has overtaken Sarai's life. Her dreams are trapped in a spermatic web of confusion. She begins the long tedious climb up the hill of redemption. Each step a triumph, each step the shedding of old life. It is the prologue to her recovery.

June 15, 1993: 6:05 a.m.

Sarai Chameleon hums to the last few notes of Miles Davis' classic 1958 *Kind of Blue* CD. She presses down gently on the hand-crafted and beveled silver stick extending from the ignition of her powder white Arnage Bentley convertible. Signaling a left turn, she pulls into the private parking facility two blocks from her plush third-floor, four-thousand-square-foot office suite that she personally designed in an urban funk decor of exposed sand-blasted brick walls. Its twenty-foot high white-washed windows offer a view of vintage downtown Birmingham. It is as trendy as one can get a hundred and twenty miles outside of the Georgia belt and two hundred miles from the bosom of the Tennessee border.

Unbeknownst to most, Alabama is the best-kept secret in style, cost of living, and accessibility to major throughways like Atlanta and Nashville's downtown districts. These localities are quintessential for surrounding metro cities that desire to wean off the tit of the two mothering states, thus branching out on their own in economics, entertainment, and community development. Birmingham is on the move, growing by leaps and bounds in leadership, innovation, philosophy, and young Black money. Chameleon Enterprise has every intention of capturing a large chunk of Birmingham's success over the next few years. Sarai is vast in money and connections—and not just any connections, but the right ones.

Slipping a folded five-dollar bill into parking slot fifty-six, Sarai begins her routine walk toward her office complex. According to the rusted billboard hanging above the parking facility advertising the latest diet capsule, it was now six fifteen a.m. and sixty-eight degrees.

"I'm making good time!" she says to herself. "The conference isn't till nine o'clock, which gives me plenty of time to prepare." Sarai tightly wraps her arms around the upper part of her body, shielding herself from the cool breeze of the early morning. She consciously tries not to wrinkle the sleeves of her cream summer linen wrap dress. It's not quite cool enough for a jacket, and the breeze a welcome comfort from the ninety-eight-degree afternoon heat.

"Good morning, Mr. Ross," she says with a warm smile.

"Good morning, SC! How are you this Friday morning?"

"Fine."

"Will it be the usual?"

"Yes, sir."

Mr. Ross owns the vendor cart two blocks from Sarai's office where she purchases her morning low-fat mocha latte and cheese scone every Friday. He is a sixty-year-old deacon at Sarai's church who wears a 1965 engraved afro, tall and unkempt, with his beard worn in the same manner. They met one Thursday evening while attending revival. Sarai overheard him telling their pastor about a tax break initiative that the state of Alabama was implementing to get more businesses to lease space in downtown Birmingham. He, of course, heard this privileged information from one of his long-time white clients. A few months later, Sarai acquired her office, along with the friendship of Mr. Ross.

"Not too much sugar—a girl has to watch her figure."

"Okay, SC." He obliges her request and wipes his hands across his shirt, already well-soiled from this morning's breakfast rush. Mr. Ross wears the same thing every day: a crisp white cotton short-sleeve shirt, slightly yellowed from too much starch. The shirt stretches tightly across his chest like a window shade that doesn't quite fit right, leaving a slice of his apple-shaped tummy exposed. His size thirty-eight Sears catalog blue jeans fasten under his belly button because his forty-two-inch waist can no longer accommodate years of Italian Genoa salami, prosciutto ham sandwiches, and cannoli from Mrs. Morahan's New York–style bakery on Thirty-Second Street.

He hands Sarai a grandee paper cup of coffee and a white vendor bag, slightly stained from the pastry. The usual also includes a daily devotional from scripture, protected by wax paper, that he tucks into Sarai's bag. Every Friday he picks a special word just for her.

"Here you go, Mr. Ross." Sarai hands him six fifty in exact change.

He smiles. "Thank you, hon." The line is long, and he is pleased not to have to make change. Mr. Ross peeps around Sarai, shaking his head in disbelief. "My, my, darling, look at all them folks. God is certainly good!"

"Yes, He is." Sarai turns to face a sidewalk already stained with elongated shadows of maxed-out blue-collar 401K patrons rushing to work so they can head home for an early weekend.

"Have a great day, SC! See you in church Wednesday night for Bible study, right?"

"Absolutely." Sarai believes God planted Mr. Ross on Kate Street to be her guardian angel.

Mr. Ross puts the money in his apron, small bills first, all facing the same direction. What Sarai *thinks* God has done, Mr. Ross is more than certain of. He turns his back to his hungry supporters and prepares a new pot of java. *Well, Lord,* he thinks,

I figure it's time. I can feel it in my soul. Make sure You take care of her. She's special and I know Your right hand is upon her. I'll continue to pray. He tosses around loose change in his side pants pockets as he waits for the coffee to finish brewing. *Yes, sir, I will continue to watch and pray.* He turns to assist another customer while Sarai stuffs the receipt from her purchase in her purse.

Out of the corner of her eye, she sees the *Montgomery Chronicle* jutting out from a metal rack just below the mints and Hershey candy bars. "Chameleon" was all that was visible from the headline. Not knowing what to expect, Sarai nervously slides over the *Birmingham Constitution* that hid the rest of the heading. "Chameleon Enterprise Ranks Number 1!" A rush of excitement touches her from the crown of her head to the soles of her feet.

"I will take this newspaper, Mr. Ross!" She digs to find fifty cents at the bottom of her purse. She gladly pays and hurries along the two blocks to her office.

I can't wait to read the article. I hope they were kind! From a distance she can see 219 KATE STREET, etched in black overlay framed by a four-by-four gold metal plate on the glass door leading to her office complex entrance. Checking the time, she admires her three-thousand-dollar Cartier watch that she recently purchased in celebration of the major contract her company won from Tokyo Software. With excitement, she ponders to herself, *No one should be in the office. It's way too early for that. I can read in peace and quiet without interruptions.* She folds the paper under her arm and walks briskly, sporting custom-made black Italian leather heels. With the shoes strapped tightly around her ankles, she eventually slows her gait so as not to break a sweat.

Arriving at the door, Sarai punches the four-digit code on the silver keypad box embedded in the brownstone brick building. The glass door opens, and she hurries past the elevator and receptionist desk straight to the stairs. Upon reaching the third floor, the words CHAMELEON ENTERPRISES are scripted in large black letters across the caramel-colored wood door leading to her company's office, a visual reminder of her success and family heritage. The office is still lit up from last night's preparation for the press conference celebrating the company's growth over the last three years. The press should arrive around ten this morning. White roses fill the office in clear A-line vases. Sarai bends over to smell the flower arrangement on her secretary's desk. *Mmm, how sweet.* Proudly, she surveys the room and sighs with delight. *Simple, yet elegant. I like it. I hate balloons and crepe paper. It is so ultra-tacky!* She laughs, knowing she sounds like a typical snob and checks herself before someone else does.

She continues down the wide hallway, pausing at the main meeting room. She grins with approval when she notices the caterers decorated the tables for the buffet with matching white linen cloths. Her choice in chefs is Miguel Ramos from Hacienda Heights, California. She wanted stylish, eye-catching yet tasty foods that would dazzle the sophisticated tongues of those attending the event. He was sure to deliver.

The PowerPoint presentation was cued up in conference room two, where the press from Channel Five would gather in a few hours. A few feet down the hall, she turns on the light in her private office suite, bringing life to the cherry red walls. She inhales with excitement.

"Wow . . ." She is left speechless at how beautiful the white roses contrast against the red walls and exposed brick. Words eventually find their way to her lips. "Electric . . . absolutely breathtaking!" She is pleased that her designer surprised her and decorated her office as well. She does a quick spin to reaffirm that there is not another soul in the office, and it is music to her ears to have a few moments devoid of daily water cooler chatter. Her only audience is the waffle cut beam lighting in the ceiling. Its reaction to her presence is a flutter of halogen light. As she heads toward her desk, she listens to the tapping of her shoes against the glazed hardwood floors.

"Call my cell phone when you get in the office," was posted on a yellow note stuck to her computer monitor. The writing was familiar. "Why does Renee want me to call her this early in the morning?" she mumbles. Sarai hits the number one on her desk phone to speed-dial Renee's cell phone.

"Renee?" Sipping her latte, Sarai paces toward the window to take a quick glimpse of the sun settling comfortably into the day. "Good morning. I got your message."

"Hey, girl."

"Renee, I've got to tell you, the office looks fantastic!"

"I thought you would like it." Renee smacks her lips together, evening out the matte plum lipstick she had just applied. "I know your taste, my dear."

"Yes, you do." Sarai takes another sip and heads toward her desk to take a seat.

"Hey, I just wanted you to know I was headed to the office."

"What? Why?" Sarai turns on her computer. "It's six thirty in the morning. I thought you would be exhausted from being at the office so late last night. I figured you would want to sleep in."

"I'm too excited to sleep. Besides, Marcus's mom has the kids. He has been up since five o'clock preparing to take our clients to the airport. Hold on, Sarai!" Renee avoids ramming her car into the back of a yellow school bus while yanking rollers from her hair. Sarai bends toward the speakerphone to make sure Renee hears her clearly. "I have told you about trying to multi-task while driving. I can hear you fumbling with those silly rollers in the background. Surely you can do your hair before getting behind the wheel."

"I have gotten a little better. Your lectures have not been in vain. Don't worry, I will be careful. The limo is picking Marcus up at our house in an hour. I thought you might need a little assistance getting ready for your big day. Are you excited?"

"Yes, but nervous. Where are you?"

With a push of her finger, Renee raises the window of her Navigator, drowning out early morning traffic and noise from the construction on 65 South. "I'm getting off the expressway right now. You will do fine." Renee puts on her blinker and moves into the far-right lane. "I'm about five minutes from the office. I will see you shortly." Renee hangs up without waiting for a response.

Sarai takes a deep breath and exhales. "Oh well. I could use the help."

"You've got mail" flashes on her computer screen. Pleased to know that her girl would be in shortly to assist her, she ignores the e-mail prompt and shifts all her energy toward the wrinkled newspaper. Sarai scans the table of contents for the page listing of the article on Chameleon Enterprise. She reaches for her cup, surprised to see she has already guzzled half of her warm beverage without food in her stomach. She digs into the vendor bag, but instead of breakfast, she pulls out the scripture Mr. Ross had given her.

"Hmm..." Each word absorbs her attention as she reads the verse:

> But he knows the way that I take. When he has tested me, I will come forth as gold.
> (Job 23:10)

"I wonder what that means." Just as soon as she read the text, it is as quickly forgotten. She sticks the scripture in the drawer where all the countless other notes and folded wax papers from Mr. Ross have retired.

Sarai hastens to the article about her company. *Let's see . . . Page three, Section 1A. What does the press have to say about us?* Sarai turns on the tasteful lamp hovering above her head, shedding a soft glow on the paper beneath it. Leaning back in the old leather chair passed down to her father by her late grandfather, she begins to read the article. After reading only the first sentence, she jolts straight up in her chair. The article is brief and cold. The author questions whether Chameleon Enterprise can maintain its growth.

The biting words plant doubt in the readers' minds regarding her business capabilities. The article begins with a question:

> Steady first-quarter earnings rank Chameleon Enterprises as number one, but is Chameleon Enterprise really a solid company? Is the company full of smoke from the exhaust fumes of the Chameleon empire founded by Joe Chameleon, Sarai's great-grandfather? Can Sarai, who has very little experience, manage a successful enterprise like the company her great-grandfather and grandfather built? As of today, her savvy father, Mr. Robert P. Chameleon, who has proven his abilities as a financial mogul, maintains the family fortune. Over 100 years of combined experience cannot be overlooked by top investors and analysts. However, can she survive in a software industry that is now dominated by US offshore investments filled with cheaper Asian and Indian engineers? Will her company be dead in the water like most young start-up companies in the next few years?

The article is full of references to the success of the men in her family, but the writer brutally criticizes her chance of survival in a white, male-dominated arena. The writer accuses Sarai of riding the coattails of her family's empire, adding little background information on her education, and throws in some numbers on the company's annual earnings from last year. The article goes to extremes to make her look bad to the public, stinging her ego in the process.

"Oh, my Lord!" Sarai slams the newspaper down on the desk, knocking what was left of her cash-and-carry breakfast to the floor. Totally wiped out from the editorial, Sarai rests her face in her hands, now heated from disappointment. *Maybe I should have waited until after the conference.* After a few minutes of silent debating, she decides her efforts would have been in vain. She knows the press may question her in the interview this morning. Instead of wallowing in what she read, Sarai decides this is an opportunity to be prepared. There is nothing worse than being caught off-guard in an interview. She'll be ready for them.

However, the harsh words left a burn on her spirit. Disturbed by the negative press, Sarai heads toward a small yellow couch on the opposite side of her office. *I just need to rest my eyes. Lord, I'm so tired of dealing with these press attacks. I have been nothing but kind to them. I have granted interviews and extended invitations to various newspapers and radio stations. Our company has had an open-door policy toward the media, but look how they've treated us! I can't process this right now.* Sarai lies on her back across the length of the couch, staring up toward the ceiling. She debates if she should counterattack the article in the conference today before the media questions her, or simply ignore the comments from the editorial.

Ten minutes into her internal deliberation, Sarai starts to drift off. Her sleep is interrupted by Renee rushing through the door with a poppy-seed bagel stuffed in her mouth, her heels in one hand, and a briefcase stuffed with documents from the contract agreement with Tokyo Software in the other. Renee is surprised to find Sarai lying down when there was so much work to do in preparation for the event. She plops her shoes on the floor and swallows a bite of the bagel that she helped herself to from the office refrigerator down the hall. There was no time to stop for apple-smoked bacon and a fresh croissant with apple butter jam, which is her favorite. A day-old bagel would have to make do this morning.

"Hey, sweetie. I thought you would be going over your speech. Why aren't you preparing? You only have a couple hours."

"I just need to rest for a minute." Irate by the questioning, Sarai puts her right arm across her closed eyes. That was a sure sign she did not want to be bothered.

Over the years Renee has grown accustomed to the body language and the proper response to each mood. "Okay, that's fine. We still have time. But I just talked to you less than fifteen minutes ago and you were hyped and ready to go. What's up?"

Renee puts her briefcase down on Sarai's desk. As she bends down to slip on her mules, she notices the newspaper next to Sarai's untouched breakfast and begins reading the article circled in red.

"I see."

Renee tosses the paper in the trashcan and turns toward her friend. "Look, not everyone is going to like you or the position your company is in right now." She takes a seat on the edge of the desk and folds her arms over her chest. Frustrated with Sarai's notorious mood swings, she ponders how to work around the unexpected situation. "That's politics, and this town is built on it. You're in a lot of folks' pockets right now. The economy has hit some businesses hard, and here comes this new kid with limited experience who has turned the business district of this city on its tail. No matter how often you bat your pretty eyes and extend your hand, the press can be bought; you know that. You know how the game is played. They will turn on you for the right dollar amount or the right positioning."

Walking over to where Sarai is laying, Renee covers her with a summer cotton throw from the arm of the couch in an attempt to console her. "You've got to be strong. This is not the time for you to break down."

Sarai brushes Renee off and turns her face toward the wall. "Turn my light off when you leave, please. I don't want to be disturbed, okay?"

"Sure." Renee knows when not to push her friend, who is also her boss. "I'll wake you in thirty minutes and hold your calls. The switchboard is already starting to light up and it's not even seven o'clock. I put your makeup bag on top of your desk so you can freshen up. Company B Designs delivered your suit around four thirty p.m. yesterday from the boutique in London. Jackie ran down to the cleaners to get it steamed for you before she left the office last night. It's hanging in the closet. Also, Marcus said call him immediately after the press conference." Renee gently shakes her friend to make sure she is listening. "Are you paying attention, hon?"

"I heard you, Renee."

Sensing the agitation in her boss' tone, she backs off. "Fine, I need you to be ready in exactly one hour. That means fully dressed. Sarai? You hear me? I don't have the patience for you to throw a tantrum on me right now. This press conference is very important to all of us."

"Okay, okay. Turn off the lights and close the door behind you! I will be ready. I am always ready. Jesus!"

Hurt about being Sarai's punching bag, Renee turns off the lights and slams the door behind her. She doesn't have the luxury of squandering the morning by moping. She heads toward the main office to make sure everything is in order for the day's events.

Sarai begins to dream again.

Which way to go? No response. Colossal cedar trees hover over her, suffocating her with their canopy. Their limbs mimic arms bent on a woman's hips. The trees begin to change shape. They sway back and forth in the night wind like men with big fat bellies full of laughter. Bending forward, then snapping backward, bursting forth with snickering conversation.

"Look at her—she doesn't know who she is!"

Just ahead, a river of broken glass rages by with dislocated cedar limbs caught in the current. The waves of shattering glass crash down with a loud force and an unbearable sound. The breeze from the cool night air is unkind to her already chafed face. The north ushers in a gentle wind that mutes the jaded voices of the night. A subtle message rises across the currents of broken glass. The message is just a whisper, but the lingering words stimulate her ears, and she yearns to hear more. She receives it and it shakes her bones, pushing her eastward and knocking her to the ground. Her ears devour the sweet nectar of the message, but it leaves bitterness in her belly. She rises to her knees with vomit spewing from her mouth, leaving her gasping for air. She perches herself against an old oak tree, comforted by the west winds. She gathers herself together and heads south toward the beckoning of the soft, still voice now speaking to her heart.

She follows the brightness of the moon and when she can't see anymore, she rests. When the sun rises, she sojourns her way home.

"POW!"

"You're dead, Sarai, if you don't do what I say."

Her menace is standing in the shadow of a filthy alley laughing at her, his face contorted with hate and distain.

"It's five after eight, Sarai. Wake up. Are you all right?" Renee pushes the control button that raises the cracked salt-and-pepper-style Chinese blinds. Immediately, rays of sunlight flood the dark office.

Still dazed from the dream, Sarai is startled and briefly unaware of her surroundings. The familiar sounds bring her back to reality. She remembers it is Friday and that in less than an hour the world will know who she is.

Renee is still annoyed by her best friend's behavior and busies herself with straightening up the office. She figures an apology will be forthcoming and decides to break the mood with small talk. She begins to stuff pencils and pens into a promotional cup that was purchased for today's festivities. While shuffling through old memos on the edge of Sarai's desk, she vacillates on what to say.

"I can't believe how it rained last night. I love the scent of a rainfall against the asphalt after a hot spell. It's the pulse that drives the city, you know?" Renee determines it would be best if she keeps the conversation bland and superficial. "I remember a great poet describing the effect as 'hazy steam boiling up from otherwise boring gray cement but mixed with wet gravel and falling leaves grinded by busy patrons going to and fro, was nature's deodorant for man's decay from building too much and too quickly." Renee laughs. "I could not have described it better myself! The weatherman said it was going to be hot and humid today. Hard to believe it could turn out to be so warm after such a cool morning."

After no response, she walks over to see what is wrong with Sarai, who is now sitting up on the couch with her head between her knees and her hands wrapped around her ankles. Renee cautiously sits down beside her and strokes her hair away from her face. The routine is familiar and usually raises its ugly head during Sarai's anxiety spells. Renee is careful not to upset her more.

"You're sweating and shaking . . . are you okay?"

Sarai looks up. "Just a bad dream and not enough sleep. I will be fine in a few minutes."

"Look at me, Sarai." Renee puts the back of her hand against Sarai's forehead to make sure she doesn't have a temperature.

"I'm okay! Stop fussing over me!"

Renee ignores the attitude and removes her hand only when she is comfortable that her temperature is normal. Unspoken, both know that their love for each other supersedes the boss-employee relationship.

"It's this project. It has taken up a lot of my time."

"You sure it's not the article, sweetheart?"

"Well, maybe a little. I think all of it just hit me this morning and you're right, the article did not help. I haven't been taking care of myself like I should." Before the words exit her own mouth, Sarai knows she is just feeding herself lies. With life she has learned that excuses excuse her right out of opportunity. Self-deception is a terrible and difficult arena to fight in. After all, who could be victorious fighting against themselves? A worthy opponent versus a worthy opponent was a guaranteed technical knockout.

"I keep having bad dreams. I can't recall the last time I had a decent sleep," Sarai continues.

"Marcus and I have been telling you for months to slow down." Renee folds the throw and places it back on the couch. "Well, you can afford the time off now. I don't want to see your butt back in this office for a couple of days—I don't care if you *are* the head woman in charge!"

Sarai puts her arm around Renee's waist. She realizes she had taken her fears and doubts out on her friend and needs to apologize for her foolish behavior.

"I am so glad you are in my life. You are as precious as a diamond. Do you know how priceless your friendship is to me? I love you. From my heart, I love you."

"I love you too, Sarai."

"I'm sorry for my behavior this morning. I know you were only trying to help."

"Mmm hmm." Renee smiles, glad that the episode has dissipated. "I forgive you for the hundredth time." Renee pats Sarai's knee. "Come on, hon, I need you to get dressed. Everyone will be here in about forty minutes, including Channel 5."

Renee grabs Sarai's hands, hoisting her to her feet. "Listen. Let me be the first to officially congratulate you. You should be proud." Sarai puts her head on Renee's shoulder and sighs. "Come now. Don't worry so much about what others think." Renee gives her best friend a long hug. "Hey!" She cups Sarai's face with both hands. "You have worked my nerves day in and day out for this very moment! Three years of long hours and cold leftover pizza from lunches that never happened because we were too busy to even stop to eat. Remember those days?"

"Yes. How about just last week?" They both laugh.

"We shall see many more long nights together, beautiful. This is it—the beginning! A major turning point for you. At times it's been a rough climb. I doubted it myself if this company would make it through those first couple of years, but this is what you have worked so hard for, and it has paid off."

Sarai laughs and takes in a lungful of air, breathing in confidence and releasing all of her concerns. She wipes the tears from her eyes. "Thank you. I don't know what I would do without you and your little pep talks."

Renee winks and points to the closet.

"All right, all right. Let me get dressed!"

8:20 a.m.

Sarai wrestles with the plastic garment bag from the cleaners, which is plagued with numerous stickpins. "How long was I asleep? I felt like I was out for a long time."

"Actually, not long. From the hallway I could hear you moaning and talking, so I thought you had gotten up. When I came back you were murmuring in your sleep. From the expression on your face, I assumed you were having a bad dream and I started to wake you. Can you remember the dream?"

"No, not really. I'm not sure if I could make sense of what I do remember."

"Well, fortunately there is plenty of time to get dressed. It will take a minute for the press to set up their equipment. That's who called early this morning asking for access to the building."

Sarai finally conquers the plastic hanger and flat-tip pins. "Who did they send from Channel 5?"

Renee prepares a fresh pot of Godiva Brazilian blend and props herself against the counter in Sarai's office to wait for the coffee to finish brewing. "His name is Terrance Rutherford. He's relatively new to the media, but I heard he is sharp. They faxed his bio last night. He did his undergraduate studies at Vanderbilt in Tennessee, and his graduate studies in Atlanta at Georgia State. Worked for a while with public access television and spent the last two years working as an investigative reporter for the morning addition in Huntsville, Alabama. Two weeks ago, he took the position with Channel 5 as an investigative reporter. Not a whole lot of investigating, I would assume, in Huntsville." Holding out a steaming mug, Sarai takes the coffee with both hands.

"Thank you."

"You're welcome." Renee pours a cup for herself and adds a hint of cinnamon. "He's done pieces on whose magnolias and azaleas have the biggest blooms, your run-of-the-mill peeping tom story of some boy being chased away from the girl's dormitory of the local college, and some kid that came into puppetry and curiosity got the best of him. Not major headliners but, according to his references, Terrance is perfect for stories with a small-town flavor." She stirs the brown powder as it dissipates into the creamy dark liquid blend and wipes the swizzle stick across her lips. "He should give our company a good write up. Besides, Marcus told me this morning that they were fraternity brothers. Apparently, they pledged the same year."

"Really? I don't remember that name at all from our time in graduate school." Sarai stops and quickly goes through an imaginary Rolodex for faces of mutual friends and acquaintances from school. "I thought I knew all of Marcus's fraternity brothers. Some of his friends I would have forgotten—there were so many—but not a frat brother. You said Terrance Rutherford, right?"

"Yep."

"Georgia State?"

"Yep."

"I'll have to ask your husband about that one. Not sure how he managed to slip by me. Investigative reporter . . . what is he doing here? This is hardly investigative news."

"He is double-dipping for Cheryl, who is out on extended leave."

"Yeah, I forgot she's out on maternity leave. Wait a minute—I forgot all about her shower! Did you?"

"Yes, yes . . . I knew you wouldn't remember. I sent her a white rocking chair I ordered from Neiman Marcus and had it delivered to her house with your name on it."

"Thanks. You're a lifesaver." Sarai swoops up her shoulder-length auburn hair into a bun and sticks several brown bobby pins in place to hold the style. "I have to make a mental note of that, so I won't forget and sound silly when she calls."

"Speaking of, don't forget you have a dinner engagement with Cheryl in two weeks. She already sent you a thank you card. It's in a pile on your secretary's desk with about forty other cards you need to read and respond to."

"I'm not going to remember that," Sarai hints.

"I will write it in your day planner right now." Renee pulls a black diary-style notebook from the desk drawer and adds Sarai's appointment. The hand carved Mont Blanc pen she uses was given to her only a few days ago as a gift in celebration of her and Marcus' three-year anniversary.

Renee tops off her coffee and checks the time on the microwave. "If we don't speed it up, we will be heading toward unfashionably late."

"I will be ready in fifteen minutes." Sarai pulls the dress from the bag and stands frozen in place. "Renee, hold up, this is not the suit I ordered. I realize I have been busy, but I was not fitted for a green suit. Where did this green suit come from?" Sarai hands the bag to Renee and checks the closet to see if there's another bag that Jackie could have possibly picked up. Surely this is an error. Sarai shuffles through layers of promotional and purchased attire hanging in her closet. Baffled, she turns to Renee. "Company B sent this?"

"Yes. Heleana personally delivered it yesterday around half past four, but at the time I was too busy to check the garment bag. I handed the bag to Jackie and asked her to take the suit to the dry cleaners for steaming. There has never been a problem before, so it didn't dawn on me to check the bag."

Perplexed, Sarai examines the suit inside and out. "I was fitted for a beige suit; the style I selected was totally different. They fitted me for a long skirt and an A-line tailored suit coat that fell to my mid-calf. This is a short skirt and a fitted jacket."

"Are you sure this is not what you selected?"

"Am I sure? Renee, you know I hate green on me! It flushes out my skin tone."

"Tell you what. I can run down to the boutique; it's just two blocks from the office. Let me get the designers on the phone. There must be an explanation. I can be back in minutes. Go ahead and start putting on your makeup and by the time I get back, you will be ready to slip on your suit."

"I don't think so, Renee. Forget it; it's too late now. I don't want to take the chance. I will just have to wear it—that is, if it fits." She holds it up under her chin and stretches the fabric across the front her body. "Worst case scenario, I wear the emergency suit we keep for situations like this. Lord knows I hate retail and prefer couture . . . off-the-rack just doesn't work well on me, but at least the back-up suit is practical and safe." She shuffles through the various garments, looking them up and down, and settles her gaze on the green suit. "Let me try this one on for size. Maybe the color will work since it's a dark green."

Renee crosses her fingers. "Here's hoping."

Sarai puts on the skirt and zips the side with ease. The silk cowl neck blouse is a mixture of a soft, raised, butterscotch and wine etched fabric scripted with delicate butterflies. Sarai slips into the jacket that bends as if painted perfectly to her full figure. It hugs her body as only a fine cut couture ensemble would do. It was obviously an original, tailored exactly for her.

"What in the world? It fits like a glove."

"It sure does."

"Are you certain you did not order this? How can you explain that it's tailored to your exact body measurements?"

Sarai turns to look in the full-length mirror attached to the closet door, admiring the touch and feel of the fabric against her flesh.

"Not sure." She forgets about the error; she is captured by how well she looks in the garment. "I'm sure I didn't order this, but it looks so nice on!"

"Very nice!"

"Do I have a pair of shoes that would match it?"

"You're not going to believe this."

"What?"

"A pair actually came with the dress."

"No way! How?"

"Never mind that. We do not have time to deal with it right now. I will stop by the boutique next week when I have some down time. Let us move on. Give Marcus a call in thirty minutes." Renee tosses the open toe shoes to Sarai. The only supports are twelve-inch-long sexy straps designed to wrap around her legs.

"I don't expect that the press conference will last long. Send the call from Marcus to my office. I am anxious to hear what our clients had to say. Marcus should be headed back from the airport by now. What time are our clients scheduled to depart from Atlanta International?"

"They will be boarding in about an hour, headed back to Tokyo."

"Go ahead and schedule a conference call for Thursday morning with their vice president of sales. His number is in my Rolodex." Sarai finishes tying the straps around her legs and bends down with absolute pleasure on how well they look. They even make her feel more confident. "I want to do a postmortem to see what worked with the project and what we can improve upon for the assignment. Give our new clients a couple of days to get settled and then give them a call. We want to touch base to make sure they feel confident and comfortable with the timelines and deliverables." Sarai grabs her speech from the pile of papers on her desk. "I will be sending Marcus overseas to network in a few weeks. The more presence we have the first few months of this relationship, the more comfortable they will be with our ability to deliver." Sarai takes a deep breath. "Okay, that's it for now. I will meet you in fifteen minutes."

"Got it." Renee is happy to see Sarai back to her old self. "I'll start working on this now." Renee jots downs a few notes. "I will see you shortly." Renee closes the door behind her, leaving Sarai with only minutes to prepare for her speech.

Sarai places her hand into her black lace bra and presses down on the soft caramel flesh of her right breast, feeling her heart race with excitement. She turns to view her profile in the full-length mirror. With her clammy hands trembling, she checks her body from top to bottom making sure every strand is in place and not a bulge is showing.

Get yourself together! Your face is on straight and your hair looks good, but something still doesn't feel quite right. When one could not put his or her finger on it, old folks would say it's a sign that a storm is coming—a breeding ground for expectation of the worst.

Sarai touches her lips and closes her eyes. She feels a presence, feels its wisdom, and is moved. She grabs a hold of the corner of her desk to keep from falling. *Mother, my sweet, sweet grandmother!* Warm tears stream down her face, wedging cocoa-colored, snake-like tracks in her make up. She is overwhelmed with visions of her grandmother bent over the kitchen sink cleaning wrinkled steak and collard greens for the annual fall church dinner. All the windows are open, and the view is of an old oak tree with leaves in a stew of yellow, red, and burnt orange, feeding autumn. Grandmother would say it is nothing you can see with the naked eye. It is a feeling in your bones; they cry out from way down on the inside trying to get your attention.

Grandmother would look outside as if there was something there, but there was nothing in the backyard. She would stand in silence with her hands clamped shut saying, "Yes, Lord, yes! It was the spirit of the Lord whispering secrets that were privileged to those who had his heart."

Grandmother was one who had His heart and his ear. She would turn to me and say, "Sarai, those aches from way down—deep down in your bones—are trying to prepare you for a storm, but all you can do is brace yourself and get ready to ride it out." She turned to Sarai as she sat on an old Folgers can peeling boiled sweet potatoes for her pies, and she would say, "You understand, baby?"

"Yes, ma'am." Sarai had wondered how she knew the knocking had begun a prompting that she carried with me. She did not know if she should respond to the light tapping at her heart. Grandmother answered her question before she could open her mouth.

"All the Chameleon women have it. If you listen to how it feels, it will guide and protect you. You understand, baby?"

"Yes, ma'am."

It was a year later that Sarai utterly understood that one could listen to a feeling. From the moment she had spoken, Sarai was being prepared for her grandmother's death, and Sarai's heart answered to that ache for the first time. The spirit had touched Grandmother that day; sunrise would take place soon, and she would depart to glory. It was a year exactly—the eve of the annual church dinner. Sarai had not felt that in a long time. Not since Grandfather's death a year from Grandmother's departure.

Suddenly, Sarai feels a sudden chill and begins briskly rubbing her arms but knows this is not the type of cold caused by the weather or piped forced air. *I cannot shake it. Oh, my Lord, I know something is going on, but right now it has to be forgotten. I must get through this.* She gathers her composure and touches up her face. She is pleased at how she looks. Thirty-one years of age, brown sugar complexion, a solid size 14 with full lips and hips, and a 38-inch bust line. She looks herself over, approves, and smiles. *I am ready! The negotiations have been solidified and Chameleon Enterprise is the number one Black consulting firm in the southeast region.* She does a last-minute check of her office, turns off the light, and heads to the conference.

CHAPTER II

STRAW AND HAY

"As an enemy is made fiercer by our fight, so pain grows proud to see us knuckle under it. She will surrender upon much better terms to those who make headway against her."
Michael De Montaigne

Everyone is gathered at conference room one enjoying a medley of festive appetizers, teas, and flavored carbonated water. It is 9:05 a.m. and Sarai stands at the entrance of conference room two summoning Renee, who is checking with the sound technician to make sure everything is in place for the live broadcast.

"Renee! Renee, come here."

"Please excuse me for just one moment, David." She puts her notes in her pocket and walks over to Sarai. "I'm a little busy, hon."

"I know. I'm sorry, but I want to do a last-minute check before I step in front of the camera. How do I look?"

"You look like a million bucks, if I say so myself—and I do say so! Straighten your left shoulder pad."

Sarai adjusts it. "How's that?"

"Perfect. Smile for me. You have lipstick on your front teeth." Renee pulls a Kleenex from her suit pocket and begins to wipe away the lipstick. "Here." She digs back into her jacket and pulls out a small gold tube. "Put a small amount of this Vaseline on your front teeth. That will stop the lipstick from running and keep your smile long."

Sarai obliges. "Okay, that's enough. Great. Are you ready?"

"As ready as I am going to be. Let's go get 'em!"

They head down the hall, mentally preparing for the presentation.

"Wait . . . use the back entrance to the conference room so you're not bum-rushed by everyone at the same time."

"Sounds like a good idea."

Sarai and Renee make their way toward the back entrance, but the crowd has already started to file in from the reception area.

"Congratulations, Sarai!"

"Thank you!"

Sarai leans over to whisper in Renee's ear. "Too late, love. I'll take it from here. You can finish taking care of whatever needs touching up."

"Good. We are running a little behind schedule. I asked the sound tech for a lapel microphone instead of the headset; let me see if he was able to get his assistant to locate one. See you at the podium." Renee pushes through the dense crowd of well-wishers who have formed a barrier around the woman of the moment to congratulate her. Everyone's unspoken intentions are the same: to toss their names in the hat for business favors. Renee looks back and smiles inwardly at her friend. She knows behind that quiet demeanor and those inviting eyes is a sharp businesswoman who understands that not everyone is worthy to sit or eat at her table. One better be bringing something if he or she planned on leaving with something from Miss. Chameleon. That was the sauce that made her so deadly in negotiations. They never knew which direction she would come from, or if she was for them or against them.

Sarai begins to work the crowd in the waiting area when she hears her name being called from the thicket of people moving to get seats near the front.

"Sarai! Sarai!"

She recognizes the voice. "Over here, Jackie!" Sarai sees a dark brown arm lined with plastic polka-dot bangles waving frantically in the air above the crowd. The magenta scarf wrapped around burgundy locks forming a beehive is headed right in Sarai's direction.

"Excuse me! I said excuse me, people!" Jackie finally pushes her way through. "Whew!" She wipes the sweat from her brow with her personal stock of recycled paper towels.

Sarai shakes her head. "Every thrift shop in a fifty-mile radius of our office has to know you on a first name basis. You would swear I wasn't paying you good money with some of the getups you throw on, Jackie."

"What are you talking about?" She straightens the second-hand long khaki skirt and personal hand painted cotton blouse of Ziggy Marley plastered across her abdomen. "I know I'm looking good. Besides, I don't have the money to buy fifteen-hundred-dollar suits like you, missy."

Jackie is indeed a true tree hugger—a sort of granola, earth-loving ragamuffin formed from a test-tube. She is hardly old enough to have experienced Woodstock, and marches to a different drum. She is a self-made original and proud of it.

"Well, good morning." Jackie gives Sarai a big hug and a wide smile.

"Good morning to you, too."

Jackie is the office manager who also owns the herb store in the neighborhood. Sarai had just signed a five-year rent-controlled lease with the state of Alabama and was in need of someone to handle the day-to-day operations of the office. Jackie impressed

Sarai with her attention to detail and professionalism to those who patronized the little community store.

Jackie is a breath of fresh air to the otherwise oatmeal corporate environment; funny and colorful, like the clothes she wears. The white folks don't know how to take her, and the Black folks resent her liberated spirit. She would tell me the yokes are uncomfortable because no one wants to lay where they shit; her rawness made them confront their ancestors' ghosts and they detested it. The gravy don't know they are the gravy, and are still trying to work through being free. Her independent aura forces them to see they are very much in bondage—physical or psychological, she says it doesn't matter. The result is still the same. The methodology is the only difference. They are trapped by self-induced chains made of plastic with sixteen-digit numbers that brand them to their masters, affectionately named Economics and Debt. For me, she keeps me grounded and balanced. I love her honesty and her "I don't give a damn" manner, for it is the jolt I need in order not to lose my head in all the attention and power that comes with wealth.

When I hired her, I was in need of energy totally the opposite of my type-A personality. I would visit the store often, and Jackie would share how she was ready for a change and wanted to sell the six-year-old business. A few seasons came and went, and the two of us became respectfully familiar with each other over chai spiced black tea and chilled aloe vera, honey, and lime juice smoothies. According to Jackie, six years of humping five a.m. to seven p.m. Monday through Saturday, and six years of her husband humping the young exchange student he hired from Trinidad to be the cashier, had gotten old and the stench was inerasable. We became friends and I assisted her with marketing so she could maximize her profit line. Soon after that, I hired her as a part-time office manager. The position went full-time within a year of opening the doors of Chameleon Enterprises.

The women strain to talk and hear one another over the fusion jazz and conversation of invited guests.

"Jackie, I wasn't expecting such a large turn out! Where did all of these people come from?"

Jackie checks the syllabus from her clipboard and shuffles through a few papers. Yelling over the music and chatter from the crowd, "Almost 90 percent of the people we sent invitations to RSVP'd at the last minute. Go figure. Some are guests of our guests. Word has it that you are hot! It seems you're in the know and the talk of the town."

"Cute, but I don't think so!"

Renee rings Sarai's cellular phone. "Hello?"

"Sarai, the camera technician needs you now! We are running late."

"I will be there shortly." Turning to Jackie, Sarai squeezes her hand. "I have to go, Jackie. I will see you at the brunch. Can you grab the contracts from my desk and lock them in the safe?"

"Sure." Jackie heads back through the jungle of people and realizes something. "Sarai!"

"Yes, Jackie?"

"Congratulations! I knew you could do it."

Sarai stretches to extend a thank you, only to see the fading vision of her assistant in the cluster of employees and invited guests rushing for seats.

"Miss Chameleon . . . Miss Chameleon. This way, please." The sound tech ushers her to the platform. "I need to help you with your mic."

"Sure."

The sound technician pins a small microphone to her suit jacket lapel. "Is that comfortable enough for you, Miss Chameleon?"

"Yes, it's fine."

"Miss Chameleon," another voice says. "I will be interviewing you."

She turns toward the voice and is greeted by a tall, dark-brown man with handsome features and dreamy eyes. His voice is smooth and deep, sending spurts of chills up her spine. Pearl white teeth are complemented by a charming smile. His close-shaved head glistens under the intense lights. He is dressed in black, flared-leg suit pants, showing off a slight cuff. His pinstriped blue and white dress shirt is fashionably accompanied by maroon leather suspenders, cuff links, with a printed tie to match. He slides his hand from his pants pocket, and he extends a genuine grin and handshake.

"My name is Terrance Rutherford. I'm from Channel 5 News."

"Nice to meet you, Terrance." She thinks to herself, *Black skin has never been worn so well.* Trying not to show she is taken by this unexpected treat; she directs the conversation toward business. "I have heard a lot about you and your work. I must say, your bio reads well."

"Hope what you heard and read was good!"

"Good enough." Sarai gives a polite smile and tries to focus but is unable to concentrate. She finds herself in unfamiliar space; she likes it, but she is totally caught off guard—a sort of vulnerable girlish state of innocence. *What do I say now? What if I say the wrong thing? What is he thinking?* She prays he does not see her obvious attraction toward him. Sarai begins to nervously pull at her watch and looks around the room for bait she could toss a line to—anyone to rescue her from the awkward moment.

Silence stretches time for the flustered Sarai, but Terrance doesn't say a word. He simply smiles and enjoys seeing the private side that he is sure is not revealed to onlookers anxious to know who she is. This is what reporters kill for. Besides, there is no need for words; Sarai says it all without uttering a sound. He thinks to himself, *how priceless—she is blushing*! Those are the best moments often overlooked by men and women: the quiet attraction that leads to the chase, the energy that leaves you lost for words, remembering the scent of the person long after they have left the room and leaving you to desire more. He laughs to himself. The attraction was obvious and mutual.

"Why are you nervous? This is not your first interview, is it?"

"No, but it's the first time I have looked forward to being interviewed by the interviewer."

"What a nice compliment, Sarai." Terrance rubs his fingers across his close-cut beard, leans forward, and gazes straight through her. "I assure you the pleasure is all mine."

She quickly stammers for conversation, totally unprepared for the attention and the pulling on her heartstrings by this charming sexy man. he is suddenly swept away into memories of her first crush. His name was Wayne: Wayne Raymond Johnson. She was in kindergarten, and he was the only boy whose bike didn't have training wheels. Impressive. All the girls wanted him, but she was his favorite. She remembers receiving her first valentine cut in the shape of a heart from blue construction paper, with graffiti in red crayon: *"Will you be my sweetheart? Signed, Wayne."* Of course, his big brother, who was in the fifth grade, helped him compose this masterpiece. Shoot, back then she was in love, but today she knows that love doesn't come so easy.

Flustered and excited from dormant feelings awakened by Terrance's flattery, Sarai quickly moves her heart into defensive mode, shielding it from any unwanted arrows shot loosely by Cupid. It wouldn't be the first time she thought a man had it going on and she ended up with what she called "brown bag love" leftovers from some other woman's love gone bad, cash-and-carry, which usually amounted to accepting lunchmeat instead of prime rib—you can't bargain or make short cuts when it comes to true love; Thursday surprise—a momma's boy still harkening to his mother's call, and last but not least, the soup of the day—Mr. Hot and Spicy but everyone has had a little taste.

"Renee said you and Marcus are frat brothers."

"Yes, we are. I am sorry, Sarai. Can you excuse me for just a second? David, Miss Chameleon and I will grab a seat till you're finish wiring the sound."

"Sure, easy."

"Let's have a seat away from the crowd. They're not quite ready for us yet."

"Okay."

They head toward the conference table behind the stage.

"He called you Easy," Sarai comments, stating the obvious.

"Yes, that was my line name. It just sort of followed me from my pledging days. People say my personality is real laid back and easy to deal with." He pulls out a chair for her and positions himself across the table, making sure he has direct eye contact and an intimate view of his attractive interviewee. "Our campus did not have a lot of guys who were interested in pledging that summer, so we combined with the brothers from your school. Not a lot of guys want to pledge during graduate school. The bonding and line activity doesn't exist; just a couple of meetings and lots of historical documents to digest."

"I am surprised I don't remember you."

"Don't worry about it, Sarai. I would come on campus, take care of business, and leave. Marcus sponsored me and we stayed in touch from time to time. No big deal."

"By the way, he knows you're in town."

"Yeah? It's been a couple of years since I've seen him, and I wanted to surprise him today."

"I'm sure he is excited to know you got here safely. He read your bio last night."

"Will he be back in time for the interview?"

"No. Actually, his wife will set up a call for Marcus and I following the interview; he is still on the road driving back from Atlanta as we speak."

"It's been a long time. I can't wait to see him. I will definitely give him a call when I get settled. I'm still getting my house set up."

"How do you like our town?"

"I like it. A little slow, but not far from Atlanta, so that makes it nice." He looks up at Sarai. His eyes penetrate hers. "I have to be honest; I remember you from a couple of the basketball games."

"Really?"

"You and Marcus were always together. I was surprised to hear the two of you didn't marry."

"We were more like brother and sister. He watched out for me, still does. Did you have a chance to speak with his wife?"

"No, there were so many people when I arrived this morning. The receptionist escorted our crew and me to the conference room."

"That was Renee, his wife, who you spoke with briefly this morning."

"I didn't realize that. Well, I look forward to meeting her face to face. Based on this crowd, I don't think we will get much of a chance to speak today."

"I'm sure Marcus will be calling you for dinner at their home soon. Listen, we better head back toward the front." Sarai gets up and walks toward the stage. She can feel Terrance watching her every step.

"Sarai."

"Yes?"

"How about an exclusive? We can do lunch or an early dinner."

"Sure!" she exclaims, and then pulls back the enthusiasm to maintain her cool. "I'm out of the office next week, but we can get together after that."

"Sounds good."

"Excuse me, the two of you can take the stage now."

Terrance escorts her to the stage.

"Please stand on this black tape, ma'am. Easy, I need you to stand to her left. Cue up the lights! Sound check! We are okay here, Easy. Please look into camera four, Miss Chameleon. In five-four-three-two . . . and you're on."

"Everyone! May I have everyone's attention? Congratulations to each of you! Everyone involved did an outstanding job and came together as a team."

"Does that mean bonuses for your employees, Miss Chameleon?"

"Yes, it does. We just need our attorneys to take care of a few things and I will make a commitment to have the bonuses ready before Christmas. The successful launch of Tokyo software has laid a solid foundation for several major deals."

"What other ventures are you pursuing, Miss Chameleon?"

"Right now, as we speak, Chameleon Enterprise is in negotiations with two of the major players for the software industry in France and South Africa."

Another reporter from Channel 2 poses a question from the audience. "What about the United States, Miss Chameleon?"

"Well, market penetration is not feasible for now, however I will be flying to Washington in the next month to talk with vice chair for the committee for communication expansion. Congress is aggressively lobbying for Black business owners to have a more visible role in the software arena, and we want to make sure Chameleon Enterprise is positioned to take advantage of some of those incentives."

"Can you speak on the rumors that Chameleon Enterprise will be going public soon, Sarai?"

"That's all the time I have for now." Sarai bends over to Terrance. "Sorry. Marcus will send out a meeting agenda to discuss highlights next week. You are more than welcome to come."

"Thanks."

"No problem. I'll make sure you get a copy of the memo."

Renee steps up to the platform. "Sarai, Marcus is on line two."

"Thanks, Renee. Sorry, guys, we will keep you posted. Thanks for coming out, everyone!" Sarai turns to shake her interviewer's hand. "Terrance, it was nice meeting you."

"You as well, Sarai. I look forward to tracking your successful career."

"Thank you, Terrance. I appreciate the encouraging words."

Handing her a card, his hand brushes against hers in the exchange. "Here is my contact information, Sarai. Call me anytime." He winks and turns to gather his paperwork and briefcase. Before she is afforded the opportunity to respond, the cameraman shouts to the crew, "That's a rap! Bring down camera four!"

The employees of Chameleon Enterprise gather around to congratulate Sarai.

"Thanks again guys! You worked extremely hard. It will not go unrecognized. What time is it, Renee? 3:15? Everyone take the rest of the day off! Let me grab this line before Marcus starts tripping." Sarai heads to her office and closes the door behind her. *Yes, we did it!*

"Marcus!" Sarai takes a seat at her desk with the phone pressed against her cheek and her fingers clicking on the wood.

"What's up, girl? You kept me hanging long enough."

"Not even you can burst my bubble today, Marcus." She checks her e-mail and hits the reply icon to type a brief note to the sender. "I just received a message from our clients. Their flight was delayed, but they are about to board the plane and wanted to take a few moments to thank us for the presentation yesterday. Isn't that just wonderful? You did an awesome job. An awesome job! Way to go!"

"Yeah, a brother got skills." Marcus pulls out a hand-rolled cigar from his suit jacket and lights the tip. He takes a long drag and exhales. A far cry from the muddy back streets of Arkansas filled with shanty homes passed down from one family member to the next, strictly by code of honor. A will was unheard of in those days. Where he was from, most folks couldn't read or write. Besides, back then people were willing to take care of one another. It was simply understood. A man's word was bond, and his character was the law. Break either one, and that was a 12-gauge shotgun up your ass real quick, and a buck, two quarters, and however else you wanted to make up the difference—burial in an unmarked grave, because that's all your lousy behind was worth. Everybody else lived in old trailer homes with tin roof tops peeled back like leftover sardine cans caused by years of decay from too much rain coupled by not enough money to fix the problem. Priority was food, not a leaking roof. A bucket and rags would have to make do until the season passed.

He was the only child born to a young single mother whose peach was taken prematurely on empty promises by a local preacher's son who, by the time Marcus was born, had bitten into the sweet nectar of too much fruit and had a bounty on his head by every father, brother, and uncle west of the county line. Word has it he was escorted out of town with a one-way ticket on the early-bird Greyhound bus special, headed for Chicago, never to return south. Mother said many years later that he was found dead with his face between the breasts of some old man's young woman. His wood chuck was stiff as a board and poking up from under the sheet as the coroner removed his body hiding a single bullet to the right temple. He died as he lived: dick hard and stuck somewhere it should not have been.

I'm sure, now, he hardly thinks it was worth it, thought Marcus. Lord knows he had plenty of time to think about it, sitting in the hotbox with his daddy and his daddy's daddy's dad. Hey, that's life and it is not fair. It is not about the hand you are dealt, it's about buying a new deck so you can have all the cards to play with.

For Marcus, it was not about hard times, just times filled with priming fresh water from makeshift pumps. Outhouses and hot baths boiled in big cast-iron pots with two caps full of red Lysol to keep down diphtheria and colic caused by the rise of the Mississippi during rainy months. Sure, there were times when money was tight, but everyone saw those times, so it wasn't too hard to go through. He and his mother had lots of dinners consisting of mashed cornbread warmed with hot buttermilk and a little brown sugar. That was okay for Marcus. He did not care for meat much. One Christmas, Uncle Jerome killed the family pet pig for dinner, and he became an instant vegetarian. After that, Marcus swore off meat, and farm animals for pets.

When he was six, he and his mother were sitting down for dinner for the hundredth time. Her eyes glazed over as she stared into the yellow lump of soggy bread and finally said, "Son, it is time to go." They caught the next Amtrak train to Georgia and never looked back.

All we had was a wool sock full of silver dollars and our love for one another. No one can ever tell me what a mother's love won't do. It kept me steady through ups and downs. So here I am, Marcus Speed, the surrogate brother to Sarai Chameleon; the first graduate of my family, and the first to own a home not delivered to me on wheels. There will be no double wide specials for my children; the buck stops here! Last year I purchased a new home for my mother right down the street from mine. I have a wife who loves me and who has given me two beautiful children. One is my son whom I nicknamed Meat. Unlike his father, my boy eats plenty of it. God has a sense of humor and has certainly been good to me. My daughter's name is Keisha and was part of the package when I married Renee. Both of my kids are the apple of my eye. He takes another drag and puts out the cigar.

"Marcus, were you listening to me?"

"Yes, I was."

"Well?"

"Well, what?"

"What did our clients say?"

"It looks like we will be working together with Tokyo software for a long time. They were really impressed with you, Sarai. On the drive up to Atlanta, I did find out that they have quite an impressive network of affiliate relationships they do business with right here in the United States. We are going to have to hustle to do a lot of networking, but it will be worth it for the company."

"Great! I am so excited!"

"You should be. Let's change the subject. It's Friday, we can talk about business later." Marcus loosens his tie and runs a Beck

Ranchero Cameroon cigar under his nose, inhaling its aroma. "So, what's up for the weekend, SC?"

"Don't know yet, but your wife is looking for you to spend time with her this weekend."

"Why can't you get some business, girl, and stay out of mine? Did you tell her I was thinking about going to New York with my boys and nephew to see the Knicks play?"

"Well, I kind of did Marcus."

"Look Sarai, this is a chance for me to relax and give back to some of my family that supported me through College." "My nephew is in Kansas City and attends Blue Springs South High School."

"Yes, I remember you talking about him Marcus.

"A great young man with good grades as well, in a city gone really bad with young black men being murdered."

"This kid is amazing! He is number 72 and is now one of the Top 25 football players in the Eastern Jackson County area! He is getting Division 1 interest!"

"My nephew, Jose Smith-Jenkins, could go Pro!"

"Look out for him Kansas City Chiefs!"

"Well, good looking out for him and, I apologize."

The tickets came to the office today and she wanted to know who they were for."

"Sarai, I told you about telling her everything! I was about to call her to let her know I was flying out tomorrow. I already purchased two dozen roses to keep the yelling down. See how you be messing up my plans!"

"You shouldn't be doing stuff behind her back! Besides, the game isn't till Tuesday."

"That's what I get for marrying your best friend. I should have learned from dating your girls when we were in college."

"Come on, Marcus. Be fair. Renee has been so swamped with the kids and helping me out here at the office. Why don't you guys go to my cabin for the weekend?"

"Did you tell my wife I would take her to the mountains this weekend?"

"Your mom said she would be more than happy to watch the kids."

"Sarai, you have gone too far! You and that wife of mine are always planning things behind my back."

"Well, don't go then!"

"I have to go now. If I don't, she will hold out on me for the rest of the year! You know how y'all do it."

"You'll love it. The air is crisp, the sky is baby-doll blue during the day and jet black at night. The stars look like diamonds, and you can just pick one right from the sky."

"You read too many romance books. Brothers do not roll like that! It would be just fine with me renting a movie, getting some hot wings and a bottle of Riesling. Do you know how many hours I have put in to close this deal, Sarai? I'm tired and I just wanted to chill tonight and catch an early flight to New York to hang with my friends for a few days."

"I'm sure Renee will appreciate the down time with you. Look, Marcus, you can take all of next week off. All I need you to do is make sure the contracts are straight and reviewed by our attorneys before sending copies to our clients. Oh yeah. I need you to send out highlights from the presentation. Also, send a copy to Terrance."

"That's fine, Sarai, but I am taking all of next week off!"

"That's fine. I can handle it."

"How did the interview go?"

"It went well. Terrance is a nice guy. You and I need to have a long talk, Marcus. I don't remember him from school."

"You don't know everybody, Miss Busybody."

"Anyway, he will contact you when he gets settled."

"Good. I look forward to hearing from him. We have a lot of catching up to do. It's been a long time. Where is my wife?"

"Doing some last-minute clean-up around the office. She is about to leave to pick up the kids."

"Tell her I said to give me a call in ten minutes so we can talk about this trip. I'm going on to the house. Hold on, Sarai, I have another call coming through."

While on hold, Sarai reflects on her friendship with her girl Renee. Every woman should have some cream for her java; just a dab will do yah. Its effect is warm liquid to the soul. Renee is the spice, the seasoning in mine; though I must admit it was not that way when we first met. She was like ice eaten too fast, leaving a harsh cold numbing effect. The streets of Jamaica Queens, New York, were her teachers and they instilled a strict raw edgy doctrine of survival: by any means necessary.

Renee is a fiery, red cropped haired, gator green-eyed, hot-tempered Irish Catholic girl who spent many years peddling packs of off-brand cigarettes (with a marginal markup for herself) to students and nuns at the elite girls boarding school of Rochester, New York. She used the money to finance her unscheduled and unpaid trips back home. She was a graduate, with honors no less, and the streets called upon her often for frequent visits to keep what she had learned sharp.

Her father was an aging gangster in a time spent out on man's craving for ten-dollar highs and speakeasy joints where you could shake down the owners for a cut of the booty. It was a new era where man's appetites called for higher quality, and supply had to meet the demand. It became a young man's scene. Enthusiasts had big dreams of upward mobility in a now billion-dollar drug industry where the return could be great, but the mortality rate even greater. Her father was too old and tired to compete. He had been wise with his blood-earned money and figured he could offer a sacrifice of repentance for all his wrongs to God and society by sending his only child far away from the life he lived. Little did he know that God could not accept these strange goodwill offerings. Society would reject his daughter, who sucked greedily from life and had gotten fat and lethargic from the generational behavior of her family's flamboyant, excessive history.

Renee had become a very bitter and resentful woman who only wanted the love and attention of her father. Fruit doesn't fall far from the tree, and Renee made a lot of jam from what she learned. It cost her five years in Bedford Women's Correctional Facility for racketeering and money laundering—a drop in the bucket compared to what she should have gotten. Her father hired the best attorney money could buy. They managed to seal her court records, giving her a blank sheet of paper to start over. Upon release, she made her way to the bus station ten blocks from her family's home and retrieved cash that was stashed in an orange rented locker during her incarceration. She took two thousand of the twenty thousand dollars, put it in an unmarked white envelope, and placed it in the church offering plate as gratitude for the four gray-haired old ladies that sat on the front pew and saw fit, for whatever reason, to pray for her from the time she was old enough to take communion. Hindsight and five years of doing nothing brought her to the understanding that those prayers kept her from getting killed. Renee then headed to a local 7 Eleven, walked over to the map section, closed her eyes, and where she lay her index finger was where she was headed. That's right: Birmingham, Alabama, the magic city!

Lord knows I had no idea what I was getting myself into when I unlocked the door and let her in. She was on her way to an interview as an event planner and coordinator for corporate functions at ETG INC. She had gotten on the wrong bus and came into our office complex for directions. In brief conversation, I intuitively knew she was a person who made things happen; she took life by the jugular. I was still putting my staff in place and took the opportunity to offer her five thousand dollars more than the job she was interviewing for. It was worth every red cent. I knew she was about to sit down with my competition. It took about a year for me to gain her trust and then I felt led to ask her to attend church. She attended early worship and was amazed by the presence of the Lord. No one ever taught her she could have as personal of a relationship as she wanted with Him. She was tired and needed His help. I knew Jesus was willing. That day she accepted Christ as her Lord and Savior. Renee has been Holy Ghost-filled, speaking in tongues, set on fire for Jesus ever since! He touched her and the real Renee arose like a dove. Six months later she gave her heart to Marcus, and they married within that same year. Marcus then adopted her daughter Keisha as his own. I am very proud of her, as she has evolved into quite the wife and mom. We have grown much together over these last three years. Renee brings a smile to my spirit, wrapping her presence around me like a fine mink coat. Anyone who is not paying attention would be caught up in her warm and comforting personality. She is like the scent left on Grandma's pillow—Chloe, Halston, or Chanel No.5. She's the familiar kiss on the forehead, Mother's silky old nightgown slipped on bare skin, bringing back many wonderful memories of being a young woman. Polyester and Olefin fabric never conjured up such wonderful images, never gave such peace, such comfort. It was like a welcome memory from days of playing hopscotch with girlfriends after school. Renee feels like those old folks that are strangers, but not strange at all. When they say, "baby come and sit a spell," they mean it, and whatever is on my mind at that moment is just as important to them as it is to me. That is Renee. The real Renee! When people meet her, they say, "Don't I know you?" She is my best friend and I love her. In addition, she takes care of my Marcus, which means the world to me. Renee says their love is sooooo good . . . like sugar, so sweet, like caramel sap from a tree, like the humming of his heart when he is standing right next to me, like when a man taps your soul, so close that in the stillness that he can hear your thoughts, *and you long "fo mo." Fill me up, Lord, with raw passionate sweet that words can't explain, the kind that makes me coo and hee hee, like the excitement felt for the first rain in the spring—a mystery, a wondrous love, Lord, that only You can usher in, born of the Spirit, a gift, soooooo good, like sugar to me, so sweet that it meets my needs.*

"I'm back. That was Renee. I will talk with you later, hon."

"Marcus, before you hang up: can we meet on Tuesday morning before you catch your flight to hang with your boys so we can finalize the paperwork and get it ready to ship over to Tokyo?"

"Yeah, that's not a problem. I can catch a late flight. I will come in early so we can knock it out. It should not take long. The final draft is done, and Jackie is taking it home to double check the figures and make sure all the signatures were signed on the dotted lines."

"Cool. Call me later when the two of you get settled."

"I'll think about it, Sarai."

"Have a great time, be safe, and kiss my godchildren goodnight for me."

"By the way, Sarai, I am keeping your Coltrane Unplugged CD. I told you it would cost!" Click.

Oh, well. The price of doing business with friends. She reared back in her aged leather chair. *The beauty of silence! I have been waiting all day to do this.* She stretches and takes in her moment of victory.

Sarai rubs the arms of the worn brown lounger with cut patches covering the wear and tear from many years of business meetings and late nights away from the family. *Still looks and feels good, Grandpa! I can still smell the smoke from his old hand-carved corncob pipe that he got from his grandfather. As a little girl, I would flop around in Grandpa's worn-out work shoes that were ten times too big for my feet, Mama screaming that I was tearing up her freshly waxed floors. I would say, "Grandpa, how come you keep these old shoes when Grandma said you can buy you a new pair?"*

"Sarai, the best experience is the old. It keeps you rooted. Makes a person respect and appreciate the new because it costs him much to obtain the old. I have walked my life in these shoes. You think one day you will be able to walk in Grandpa's shoes, little one?"

"No sir! I don't think my feet will grow that big."

He laughs at the innocent response. "Life is hard and these here shoes keep a man humble. You never forget where you come from. Never forget the roads you walk in life." Over and over, he would tell me that story throughout the years up until his death. Well, I made it, Grandpa, and I hope you're proud of the steps I have taken.

Sarai begins to unwrap the leather straps from the four-inch heels she wore at the conference. She rubs her legs and ankles with a sigh of relief. It has been an exciting and rewarding day, but she is glad to see it conclude. With her French manicured toes, Sarai teases the mock white and black swirled chinchilla throw rug stretched neatly at the base of her chair. The sun looks as though it is ready for bed with half of its fullness covered by the evening clouds patterned in a display of cotton pink, crayon yellow, and a breath mint blue collage of symmetry and design. She notes and marvels at the paradigm of God's brilliance and mastery of art displayed differently with each passing day. How he accomplishes such greatness, man shall never know or understand from this side. Unfair, yet another example of his secrets whispered to those who have his heart. Favor is not fair and is an inherited rite of passage. Besides, Jackie, while picking at her freshly washed and massaged locks, would say that is why he created mankind last. Man would find a way to take credit for the heavens if they knew the recipe for how God mixed it and baked it. Then man would have the audacity to label it with a price tag.

Sarai swivels in her chair and gazes quickly at the bouquet of congratulatory cards and memos given from loved ones and business associates piled three inches thick in her inbox. Proud and honored, she marks a day in her planner to answer each card personally. *I let time totally slip away.* The computer monitor displays seven fifteen p.m. and she begins to shut down for a long, well-deserved weekend. It's been a busy day and Friday eve could not have come sooner. Sarai opens a desk drawer concealing files of contact information. After dropping a manila folder with phone numbers and e-mail addresses for her clients into her briefcase, she locks the drawer. *I am looking forward to doing absolutely nothing for three days.* There is a knock on the partially closed door to her office. The aroma of bitter coconut oil feels the air and, without looking up, she is aware of who it is.

"Hey, Jackie. Come on in. What are you still doing here? I just told Marcus you left hours ago. He will be in on Tuesday to help us review the contracts. I saw a few errors, but they were minor. Can you be here by seven a.m.?"

"I sure can, my dear. I was on my way out and saw that your light was still on. I thought I would swing by and drop off this package." Jackie pulls out a four-by-six box wrapped neatly in standard post office mailing paper from behind her back. She walks over to Sarai and hands her the package. "Also, here is yet another letter from your mysterious writer. A courier delivered the package a few minutes ago, but the envelope was propped up on my PBX wrapped with the same blue and cream suede ribbon. I noticed it after the conference. That envelope was not on my desk prior to the meeting. I believe your mystery writer was here today. This is your third letter and, yes momma, I am keeping count. Hope you don't mind me peeping in on your glamorous life, but baby, I have pulled up a chair and decided to take a peek!"

Sarai rubs her finger across the suede ribbon wondering who it could be and why this person has not made himself known.

"Sarai?"

"Yes, Jackie?"

"You want to tell me what is going on?"

Sarai looks up at Jackie, perplexed by the question. "I don't have a clue. Honestly!"

Jackie lets her friend know through crossed eyes that she doesn't believe her. The proof was in the pudding: no man would put out this type of energy toward someone he doesn't know. Jackie picks up the letter and examines the words inscribed on the envelope. "I go through hundreds of letters for you every day. Granted, forty percent is junk mail, but I don't recognize the writing from any of our vendors or clients." Jackie hands her back the envelope and settles her attention upon the small box.

Sarai puts the letter down and begins to remove the packaging that is unmarked and has no return address. "The gift is probably from our client."

"The envelope says, 'congratulations' in the same writing style as the last two letters."

"Well, Jackie, let's see what's in the box first."

"Good! I love presents."

Sarai rips the paper from the square object. "Amazing. Simply amazing! What a beautiful box!" Sarai carefully hands the box to Jackie who traces her fingers over the fine etching and admires the sparkle of light with each turn.

"Sarai, this is cut crystal with an emerald chameleon carved into the top." Jackie puts the gift under Sarai's desk lamp for closer examination. "Can you believe that? Those are two diamonds for the eyes. Those guys must have spent a fortune on this gift! Someone at that company really wants to get your attention." Jackie hands the box back to Sarai.

"Yes, they do, and they have."

"What's wrong?"

"Nothing . . . just stunned. I can't imagine why they would send such an elaborate gift."

"Well, one thing's for sure: it's extraordinary! I have never seen anything like it."

"Neither have I." Sarai places the box carefully into the packaging for protection.

"Lock this in the safe for me. I'll give our clients a call on Tuesday to find out if they sent this or not."

"What about the letter, Sarai?"

"I'm not sure if I can take anything else today." Sarai stares at the white manila envelope wrapped with three fine blue ribbons neatly tied together just like the two previous letters.

"Are you going to open it or play with it?"

Sarai rubs the fabric envelope with her fingers. "Why not? Let's see what he has to say."

"Read it out loud!" Jackie covers the letter with her hand. "And don't you skip a word!"

Woman, I whispered in your ear last night. As you slept, I watched in awe. I marveled at the sight of your smile when you cooed to the sounds of my pillow talk. You didn't make a move as I played and ran my fingers through your curly locks; instead, you released a sigh and it pleased me to imagine that at that very moment, I was in your thoughts. You rested in my arms; unaware you were surrounded by peace. I held you ever so closely, making sure not to disturb your sleep. I smelled the perfume of pansies from your hair, kissed you down your arms. I noticed your sheets were pulled back and wrapped you in my robe to keep you warm. I stared at your beauty all night long and commanded the angels to sing a sweet, sweet lullaby as I watched you and asked God to protect your dreams. You arose in the morning; woman, did you notice that I was there? I stood in the entrance to your bathroom door as you lined your lips and applied your makeup with such care. Woman, I was there with you when you glided across the park. Remember the wind sending a chill up your back? Well, it was I, whispering um-um-um at the way your hips moved and the way you walked. So proud, woman. Back straight, heels clicking with every stride; Black never looked so good, woman—the light of my life. Cocoa chocolate hues of cinnamon mixed with a little attitude. Just the way I like it, brown sugar.

Woman— the reason God painted the sky a ray
of blues. Did you notice the stars I asked the Lord
to hang for you in the night? Well, you'll have to
forgive me—I felt a need to express myself for
you, so I used the heavens as a palette to write. A
love letter, woman, that would never ever die. The
heavens bow down to you, the earth gives way to
who you are, woman: the celebration of my heart.

Sarai scans the letter again and wonders how the silent penman
has viewed the crevices of her desires. Things only mentioned in
private from her soul to the Lord. *My fame is not in making a name,
but in finding love and love finding me. The courtship has begun,
and the key has been shaped from tear-stained pillows through long
cold nights void of male companionship. Those tears crystallized,
gathered, and pressed into a fine powder unlocking what was hidden.
How he knows the vacancy of my heart is a mystery. God has allowed
him to see only that which He knows. Whoever this mystery man is,
he is a treasure to behold. Who is he, Lord? Who is he that, at Your
discretion, You have granted access?*

"Oh my, Sarai. You, princess, have a secret admirer. My
word—who could it be?"

"I don't have a clue."

"Don't worry. I am sure we will be hearing from him again.
Make sure you call me if I am not around when another envelope
is delivered. If he writes like that, I can't wait to meet him.
Hopefully, he has a brother!"

Jackie looks around the office and takes a quick survey of
all the partially eaten leftovers displayed on crinkled aluminum
foil and deserted plastic disposable serving bowls, their minute
of fame gone in a matter of hours by hungry patrons devouring
them during the day's festivities. "I guess I should straighten up
the office a little. The smell of old salmon and Cuban cigars is
not a good mix."

Sarai grabs her keys and briefcase. "Let housekeeping do it, Jackie. You will be here all night trying to get this office back in shape. Besides, I know you are tired. You have worked long hours with Renee getting this conference together."

"Okay. I will call housekeeping just to make sure they come by no later than tomorrow morning. If this trash sits here all weekend, I don't want to imagine how bad it'll smell Monday morning. Are you ready to leave? You want to walk out together?"

"Yeah, let me grab my purse." Sarai retrieves her handbag from her closet.

Jackie shuffles through a variety of advertisements and mail order catalogs when she notices the red indicator light for incoming calls on Sarai's phone blinking. "There is a call coming through on line one. You want me to let it go to voicemail, SC?"

"No, answer it. It may be Marcus."

"Chameleon Enterprises."

"May I speak with Sarai?"

"Can I tell her who is calling?"

No response.

"Hello . . . hello?" Jackie looks at the receiver and hangs up. "That was strange."

"Was that Marcus?"

"Not sure. It was a male, but there was a lot of static and then the call dropped."

"Could you see where the call was coming from?"

"No, I couldn't. Caller unknown was displayed." She gathers up the books and stores them in Sarai's junk mail bin. "He asked for you, though. Hey, maybe it was your secret admirer!"

"Whatever. Let's get out of here. It could have been a cell phone and they lost the signal. If they want me bad enough, they will call back. I will meet you downstairs in the lobby. Let me grab a couple of files. I am going to be out of the office next week."

Jackie heads toward the reception area to make a quick call to housekeeping before heading to the elevator. "I will wait for you downstairs."

Sarai turns off the remaining office lights and a flickering red light catches her eye, signaling that there is an incoming call on line one again. "Who is calling this late in the evening? Should I answer it?" She rhythmically taps the tip of her car key against her computer. "It might be Marcus or Renee, but they should be heading up toward the mountains by now and that would put them out of range. And if it's them, why are they not calling me on my cell phone? I should just answer it. Hello? Chameleon Enterprises, may I help you?"

Sarai stares down at the display flashing caller unknown. Silence reciprocates from the other end of the receiver; a mysterious agenda now made clear. She sets her belongings down and takes a seat. Immediately the ache she ignored earlier encircles her, trying to forewarn her to batten down the hatch and cast her anchor deep.

"Who is this?" Sweat beads across her forehead, dripping southward into the creases of her mascara-accented eyelids. Salt from the moisture mixes with the chemicals, burning her eyes.

"Sarai? Is this Sarai Chameleon?"

"Yes, it is. May I help you?" She douses water from a half empty water bottle onto a tissue and gently rubs it across her face.

"Sarai? Please don't let this be. My, my, woman, I haven't heard that voice in a long time! You sound so good, SC!" Sarai could sense who was on the line. Cigarette smoke stifles and chokes the voice communicating over miles of copper cable linking the call, but no amount of distance could erase the familiar spirit that has clawed its way back.

Sarai could sense that he was drunker than a mosquito gnawing on the veins of a street derelict whose blood was full of cheap moonshine and rubbing alcohol. Just like a festering maggot waiting for the right environment to show how foul it can be, evil has no decorum and is rotten through and through. Satan has been quite successful, not by developing a new strategy of attack, but by mastering patience since he has nothing but time on his hands. He has taught his son well.

"I called to congratulate you! Did you get my gift? I thought the crystal box was perfect. When I saw it, I said, 'now that is Sarai!' The cost was unimportant. You have come a long way in a very short time. Yes, I am immensely proud of you."

Warm bile pumps from her stomach, filling her throat with thick foam. She closes her eyes, trying desperately to hold back the vomit. The conversation is interrupted by a long exhale by the caller. Sarai's legs begin to shake. Her strength gives way, and she places the receiver against her chest. Her heart racing violently, pounding through her rib cage. She prays that he is unable to hear its outcry of groans and pain. *Why Lord? Why now?* She remembers today's devotional: *I know the way that you take and when I have tested you—you will come forth as gold. Job 23:10.*

"What do you want? Why are you calling?"

"Did you think I had forgotten about you? Besides, we are family and I wanted to congratulate you. I must say, you looked stunning in that green suit. I didn't think the shoes would match, but I got a quick glimpse as you left the stage. They went well with the outfit, don't you think? When your office manager dropped off the beige suit for steaming, I had my assistant pick it up and swap it out for the green one I had designed for you instead. Aren't you going to say thank you?"

Sarai's unwanted invite to Hades is briefly interrupted when she hears the ringing sound of the elevator arriving on the third floor.

"Hey!" Jackie stands in the entrance to her office pointing down at her watch. "What's going on? It's eight o'clock. I came back to see what was taking so long. Security wants to lock up for the night."

"Go ahead, Jackie. I need to take this call."

"You sure?"

"Yeah, yeah, I'm sure."

Jackie can see the worry lining Sarai's face as it is magnified by the shadow of streetlights outside her window, the only supply of visibility in the entire office. "You look concerned."

Sarai quickly plasters a ghostly smile from her treasure chest of costumes she uses to mask what she doesn't want perceived. Perception is reality for those who can change quickly for each scene of life. "I'm fine. I just need to finish up this call."

"I can hang around for a while if you like."

"No, I will be fine."

"Well, you better call security to walk you out."

"I will. Thanks. I'll see you Tuesday."

"Good night, Sarai."

She listens for the fading sound of Jackie's retreating footsteps back to the elevator before resuming the conversation. "What do you want, Russell?"

"That's no way to talk to your favorite brother-in-law."

"There is no love between us, and you will never be family."

"Calm down, baby girl. Everyone is talking about your career, and I called to congratulate you. Comments from your father's circle of business associates say you will quadruple the family's wealth in less than ten years if you keep going at this pace. 'The rebirth of Chameleon Enterprise! The seed of the Chameleon bloodline is unstoppable and continues to reap a great harvest in the southeast!' You made front page, girl! You're the buzz of the town—the belle of the ball! *Black Enterprise*, *New York Times*, and *Town and Country* all want to interview your father. Damn, Sarai, you got the white and Black folks pulling their chain over you. Old footage of your grandfather aired on the local network last night."

He takes another drag from his cigarette. "So why haven't you called, Sarai—wait, don't answer. Let me guess. You have been too busy building a name for yourself. Why worry about such small trivial things like your family? I guess it doesn't matter. You have not missed much, as with any bad soap opera you can miss watching for years and pick right back up on the plot. Your fake mother has been keeping up the façade about her baby being the great daughter and how fabulous—how simply fabulous—you are. I have to give your mom props because that takes a lot of energy keeping folks' butt holes wet with lies. That tongue of hers stays lubricated."

"You are hardly in a position to criticize anyone's family, Russell. Arrogance and vanity still suit your case; I can clearly hear your love affair with the bottle is still hot and heavy. Tell me, is it still scotch?"

"Sarai, you sound bitter, hon. I thought your heart would have changed." Clearly incensed by her rebuttal, she hears him shift in his chair. She knows he's wishing he could climb through the phone to reach out and grab her. "Truth is told, you're not as innocent as you would have yourself and others believe. That's not why I am calling. I need you to come to Montgomery as soon as possible. Pack a suitcase, oh, and bring that baby blue pants suit. Coco Chanel was the designer, right? You wore it the night I gave my acceptance speech for a congressional seat representing Alabama in Washington D.C. I remember because you looked stunning. Your hair was swept up with curly locks cascading around your face, just how you wore it today. Do you remember that night?"

"Yes, I remember it very clearly, Russell. It was the night that my dreams died. You spoke five words that changed my life forever and here we are."

"Yes, here we are, Sarai. I need you to come next weekend."

"I can't."

"You have to. It's that important or I would not have called."

"I said no! You don't run my life. I am not married to you and my name is not Nayia! I am not about to drop my plans and head back to Montgomery because you called."

"Really? So, you're smelling yourself now and think you got it going on like that because you got a few dollars? Let me remind you that you don't! Your paper means nothing to me, my love. I can make or break you! Don't make me go there, Sarai! Nayia has been asking for you, by the way."

"She knows why I have not returned her calls."

"How selfish! What kind of sister are you? After all, Nayia put off her career so you could follow yours. She made the sacrifice to stay in Montgomery and help out the family."

"No, she stayed to marry you, Russell. I was not a part of my sister's career path."

"What if the press finds out that you have not seen your family in three years? Oh, I get it. The occasional call on the holidays and birthdays somehow excuses you. I can see the headlines now."

"I think the press would write the story a little differently, Russell. I have been terribly busy building a business in just over three years with little help. Maybe I will expose the real reason I have not seen my family."

"Sarai, you're on the heels of fame! Its taste is addicting, isn't it? All that power. All that wealth. All that attention you crave is racing through your blood, giving you the high you've been searching for."

"I'm not worried about you running your mouth or your silly threats."

"You just need to come home. I'm not asking. I am telling you. Don't make this difficult. I don't want to hurt you."

"You already have."

"Listen, your sister is pregnant. Sarai, did you hear what I said? Nayia is pregnant and she wants to see you. Sarai? Never mind. You don't have to say anything. I don't want to argue with you. Now is not the time to hash it out, and it will take more than this call. Believe it or not, I understand you're hurting. I know you weren't expecting to hear this, and especially not today. I am sorry that you had to learn about Nayia's pregnancy this way."

"Russell, everything revolves around you, and I don't have the energy to fight. Do you understand you are talking about another life being brought into this already disturbing situation? How could you even consider it?"

"What can I do about it now? What do you want me to do? I gave you what you wanted and now I need you to give me what I want."

"What have you given to me, Russell? You have brought nothing but darkness."

"I don't know what you're thinking, girl, but don't be a fool. You knew it was a possibility that Nayia could get pregnant. She is my wife, for Christ's sake! This is not easy for me either. Look, your father is planning a big dinner at the house for the entire family and a few of his closest friends next weekend. That gives you a week to get your head straight. We can talk more when you get in town. I expect to see you. Don't make me come and get you, Sarai. There is a lot on the line for both of our families. Don't make a decision that can potentially ruin a lot of lives! Make no mistake, I will protect my interest. By any means necessary, and I mean that.

Besides, I have an offer that you and your boy Marcus cannot refuse, and it is a deal worth millions. Marcus will eat this proposal up if given the chance to review it, Sarai."

Russell's phone line lights up and he quickly sits up in his chair.

"I got to go, talk to you soon. You better show up!" Click.

Montgomery
"Hello Mr. Garret, I was expecting your call."
"Did you speak with her?"
"Yes, sir."
"Did she accept or offer?"
"Not yet, sir, but she will."
"We certainly hope so, or your family will find you in a cold ice truck with a bullet through your head Russell!"

Sarai thinks about words of encouragement from her grandfather. In her fear, the best experience is the old. It keeps you rooted. It makes a man respect and appreciate the new because it cost him much to obtain it. Life is hard and these here shoes keep a man humble. You never forget where you come from, never forget the roads you have walked in life. Those lessons will pull you up by the boots straps when you need them. It keeps you from being swallowed up by the now. It teaches you that you can survive when you feel like you can't. You are not the source that got you through the battle in the first place. It is the hand of the Lord.

Raging waves of broken glass crash against her psyche. Confusion has bedded up his back with shackles and has come a-calling at the most inopportune time. *I have worked so hard, Grandpa. I never wanted to let you and the family down! I wish you were here!* She tears off her jacket, scattering the gold buttons and ripping a hole in the blouse she desperately wants off of her flesh. *Never forget the source of your strength, Sarai. Never forget the lessons of your past. Those lessons have their place.*

Grandpa, what do I do?

Call on the Lord, little one. Can you remember that, princess?

Yes, sir.

Good. Let grandpa tie your shoes and we will head on up to the house. Grandma is frying fish and green tomatoes. I can smell it in the air! Innocence lost is an opportunity for sin to gain ground. The rattler—a consummate salesman—is always lurking in the darkness waiting for the right moment to peddle his off-kilter remedies, placebos, and quick fixes to unsuspecting souls.

CHAPTER III

THE CEDAR TREE

*"Evil has no substance of its own, but is only the defect of
excess, perversion, or corruption of that which has substance."*
John Henry Newman

Jackie stares at the yak-blue cement pole with the number
forty-six imprinted in black signifying her parking space. She
has one foot in the car and her key in the ignition turned to
display the control panel. Wrestling with whether to check on
Sarai or not, she gets an affirmation from the plastic cow covered
in red velvet sitting on the dash. Jackie dials security and asks for
an officer to escort her upstairs.

They arrive to find Sarai facing the window. The light from
the hallway reveals her hunched over in her chair, hands gripping
the windowsill with brutal force. "Wait here, officer. I will just be
a minute." The office is dark and eerily quiet. The only sound is
the buzz from the hall's overhead light that needs replacing. "Are
you okay? I had bad vibes and came back to check on you. I just
didn't feel it was a good idea to leave you here by yourself."

Jackie turns the chair around and is startled by Sarai's appearance. The room is filled with an overwhelming odor of musk; she is thrown back by the faint smell of urine and vomit. Crushed glass is at the foot of Sarai's desk. The gift box is now a puzzle of broken crystal, its former beauty a distant memory. All that remained was the head of the emerald chameleon.

"What in the world happened? Your clothes are soaking!"

Sarai looks up, eyes glazed. "I have been running for so long. Seems like a lifetime ago when we got started." Her voice is calm and steady, as if all energy and life is drained.

"What's going on? What have you been running from? Is this about the call?"

"It wasn't much to brag about, but we built it one day at a time. I don't even know what to do. Now I may lose everything! What am I supposed to do?" She slams her hands against the armrests of her chair.

"Whoa! What are you talking about?"

Emotion mounts as Sarai struggles to breathe. Her body shakes under the weight of the stress. Soon her air passage becomes blocked as her body struggles against itself. She can only surrender to its will to let go.

"Slow down, honey, and catch your breath! It's going to be okay."

Everything goes black. As Jackie extends a hug to her friend, there is no response from the lifeless body. "Sarai! Officer, please help us! Dial 911! We need medical assistance right away! Hold on, sweetie, it's going to be okay. The ambulance is on the way." She holds her close, afraid that if she lets go, she will lose her.

"Where am I?" Sarai is rudely awakened to a deadly cocktail of used-up intravenous liquid-antibiotic bags hanging from metal trees, a recognizable smell of hospital disinfectants, and soiled bedpans as she waits her turn for medical attention on a cold gurney in an overcrowded emergency room. "My head is killing me."

Jackie extends her arm around Sarai's waist, preventing her from moving. "Don't try to sit up. Lay still, Sarai. You're at Baptist Regional Hospital. You passed out at the office. You gave me the worst scare of my life! I would smack the crap out of you if you weren't in so much pain." Jackie takes a seat next to a cart with a jungle of rubber food warmers and empty milk and juice cartons. "You had the worse anxiety attack. Thank God you're all right! I know you don't want to hear this, but now is as good of a time as any to tell you."

"Tell me what?"

"Your mom and dad are on their way to Birmingham."

"What?"

"Be still!"

"Why? Who called them? I don't want to see them right now!"

"Calm down before you yank the IV out of your arm! That is what got you here in the first place. The hospital had to get ahold of your immediate family. Your parents will be here in the morning. They wanted to come tonight, but I convinced them that you were in good hands. I don't know what is going on, but whatever it is, it's not worth your life."

"Jackie."

"Hush, Sarai, you are always doing the talking. Now you listen." Jackie grabs her friend's hand and rubs her arm to keep her calm. "I called Renee and Marcus. The doctor said he would not let you leave tonight if you didn't have someone to take care of you. They are on their way."

"I have messed up everything, Jackie."

"No, you just have some things to sort out and it will take a little time is all. I'm going into the office tomorrow to send out an e-mail letting the team know you're out on a long overdue vacation for two weeks. Marcus and I will be filling in for you. We can take care of the office; you just take care of yourself."

"Sarai!" calls a familiar voice.

Jackie turns to see a frantic male pushing his way through waiting patients to ask the station nurse for Miss. Chameleon. "Well, speak of your angel, Sarai. Your boy just showed up." Jackie waves to him. "Marcus, we are over here!"

He pushes his way past the orderlies and third shift nurses to where Sarai is resting. "Thanks for calling me, Jackie. Are you okay, baby? What did the doctors say? What happened, Sarai? What is going on?"

"Hey, catch your breath, Marcus. The doctor said she would be fine."

"I'm okay. Really."

He takes her hand as if touching her would make everything better—not for her but for him.

"I didn't mean to scare you guys."

"Let her rest. We can take a walk till the doctor is ready to check her out. Sarai, we will be right back, hon."

"Okay."

They head toward the sliding doors away from view. "Can she see us, Jackie?"

"Not from this angle."

"Good."

Marcus presses his back against the wall and grabs his head. He bends down, resting his hands upon his knees. "I wasn't ready to see her like that, stretched out on that iron bed, so vulnerable." He stands up and looks up toward heaven. "Thank you, Lord, for keeping her."

"Trust me, she looks a lot better than she did a couple of hours ago." Thinking this would be a good segue for a cigarette, Jackie searches her duffle-style carrying bag for a tobacco stick, but to no avail. She gives Marcus a few moments to gather himself and temporarily escapes into the moving wallpaper of patients being pushed up and down the hospital halls in wheelchairs by family and candy stripers. Like a silent black and white movie long spent out, she is sure they wished it was curtain call and they could bow out of this bad scene rated G for gloom. She wishes she could as well.

"Where is Renee?"

"In the car. She had to call her mom to let her know we are back."

"Good, I told the doctor you and Renee would take her back to your place to rest."

"Yeah, that is not a problem. We will stop by her house and pick up some clothes."

"I have to leave, Marcus. My children have not eaten. Call me tomorrow and let me know how she is doing, okay?"

"Sure."

"Her parents will be here in the morning. I gave them your contact information."

"It's about time they showed up."

"Not your business. We don't know the story. Sarai will work it out. You just need to be supportive, not judgmental. Ragging her about her family is not what she needs right now. Let her walk through this herself. We just need to have a listening ear. Don't pry. Let her tell us when she is ready."

"Can you give me an idea of what happened?"

"I don't know. We got a call before I left the office, but there was no one on the line, so Sarai said she would meet me downstairs. I was on my way to the elevator when I saw the switchboard light up again. I could see that Sarai picked up the phone. Honestly, I thought it was you checking in and figured she would be a few minutes. After about fifteen minutes I came back, and she was still on the phone. I had a bad feeling as soon as I walked in the room, but instead of listening to my gut, I headed to my car after she told me she wanted to finish up the call. I sat in my car for a while staring at that elevator, thinking she would be down any minute.

No Sarai, so I called security. When I came back to the office, she was sitting there crying. She had urinated in her clothes and was shaking really hard. She started murmuring about the past and the next thing I knew she was having an anxiety attack.

"Oh, here comes her doctor. Dr. Abernathy, this is Marcus Speed. Marcus and his wife are Sarai's closest friends and will take care of her."

"Nice to meet you both." He extends a clammy, pink hand to Marcus, and quickly rakes back the few strains of graying hair left on his naked head. Barely forty-five, Dr. Abernathy looks as if retirement should be an option, but emergency room care can age one quickly. He fumbles over red and green ballpoint pens lined neatly in his pocket protector, and then pushes up the heavy framed black glasses on his nose.

"Will she be okay, Doc?"

"She will be fine. Just needs to rest. I have a few forms that I need you to fill out. She will be staying at your home, correct?"

"Yes, sir."

"Monitor her for the next forty-eight hours. I would not recommend her traveling right away. She will be drowsy for the next twenty-four hours because of the medication, but she needs to sleep." He scribbles something on a small pad and hands it to Marcus. "Here is her prescription. I have already released Sarai."

"Thank you." Jackie turns toward the sound of clicking designer soles against the tiled floor. "Here comes your wife, Marcus."

Renee anxiously brushes by Jackie. "Is she okay?"

"She's fine, baby."

"I'm gone." Jackie heads back to see Sarai. "Don't forget to call me."

"What happened?"

Marcus grabs his wife's arm and heads toward the nurses' station. "Long story. Let's just get her home, baby."

⌒∞⌒

Marcus enters Sarai's passcode to the exclusively private condo community fifteen minutes from downtown. He drives by the security check and waves to the officer, who is familiar with the driver and ushers him pass the restricted gate. Preston Miller owns a major protection franchise throughout Alabama, and they play golf together once a month. Occasionally, they hook up to drive up 85 North for a Falcon's game to see their favorite teams if they happen to be playing against Atlanta. Both root for the underdogs; for Marcus it's the Saint Louis Rams, and for the security guard it is the Detroit Lyons. He curves around winding roads leading to affluent homes owned by PhD's who wrote major dissertations that funded space exploration during the mid-1960s for the aerospace center in Huntsville, Alabama. Many were retired civil rights leaders whose era had come and gone, making their money from the collection plates of the southern Baptist churches and northern politicians who paid handsomely for conservative inroads that charmed Black voters. The homes of the upper-upper echelon of the community sat up on the hill; young corporate icons that managed to build wealth from ecommerce and the scraps left from the father of Microsoft. The community is plush, comfortable, and very vanilla with a few chips here and there. Not too showy. Onlookers and perspective buyers would get the impression that they just stepped into a page of *The Millionaire Next Door*.

He pulls around into the circle driveway, triggering flood lights displaying this year's summer blooms of purple pansies, gardenias, and red roses. "Ladies, I will be right back."

Sarai yells from the car window, "Don't forget to leave on some lights!"

Ten minutes later, Marcus returns to the car, pulls out of the driveway, and heads for the highway. "I think I grabbed enough clothes. Sweats and jeans, SC, like our old college days."

"That is perfect. Thank you."

Marcus reaches over the seat and hands her an overnight bag and an envelope. "I grabbed it from the refrigerator door. It said to open immediately. Baby, please turn on the overhead light so Sarai can read the note."

Dear sweet Sarai,

I trimmed the hedges and planted new grass seed. I will be by in two weeks to finish the landscaping. The cost is one hundred and fifty dollars; just drop it in the mail. Momma Oxley baked you a cherry pie. I put it in your refrigerator. It will be nice with some ice cream after sitting for a few days. Sure miss that granddaddy of yours. Not fair he put his good foot on a cloud and rode on off to heaven still owing me twenty dollars from that game of chess in 1968. It's bad enough he got away with the most beautiful girl in all of Florida. Take care, darling.

Uncle Shivers.

Sarai tucks the note in her handbag. *How nice of him.*

Marcus adjusts the rear-view mirror so he can see Sarai. "Who was it?"

"Mr. Shivers. He was my grandfather's best friend for over thirty years. He is like family to us. He moved to Birmingham after retiring from the railroad as a porter and makes a few bucks every now and then from his first love: gardening. He and his companion, Mother Oxley, met at a colored-only boarding house in Saint Louis when his train stopped for fuel layovers before heading on to Paducah, Kentucky.

"Mr. Shivers eventually charmed Mother Oxley, and they got a one-bedroom suite on top of the chicken shack two blocks from

12th Street in Montgomery till it burned down from Uncle Shivers trying to heat a can of soup on a hot plate.

"I used to love watching them play Bid Wiz on Friday nights. I don't know what was hotter: the chicken frying below or a game of Bid from the little spot right above. Mother Oxley would cook up a pot of venison stew with some hot water cornbread. Folks would come by after a long work week and get Mr. Shivers all rallied up saying 'people from the Midwest can't play cards.' All of a sudden someone would holler out 'you and the missus better get a blanket when you catch this here train to Boston! Gonna be a long ride, so you best grab your coat!' Momma Oxley and Mr. Shivers would whip them like they stole something. Popping those cards down on the table fresh out the pack, sprinkled with a little baby powder. After the building caught fire, my father moved them into a senior citizens' retirement community here in Birmingham with some of Grandpa and Mr. Shivers' old running buddies.

"Mr. Shivers has been taking care of Nayia and me since Grandpa died. Momma Oxley has been his companion for twenty years and has baked sweets for me since, well, since I can remember. Even when she went home to St. Louis in the winter, she would send me a coconut cake in the mail for my birthday. Uncle Shivers would always write on the box 'sweets for my sweet Sarai.'

"Him and my grandpa grew up in Greenville, Mississippi, and traveled together when they were seventeen all over the south as porters. That's how my grandpa met my grandmother and he fell in love with her at first sight.

"My grandmother was hooked the first time she saw him. They used to call her 'big red' because she was so fair and stacked like a plate of pancakes. Spread like butter, not margarine, and dripping with tree maple syrup; 'rich'—that's how they described Momma Red. Anyway, soon after that, Grandpa started courting Grandma, and he had to start thinking about settling down. He started working at one of the family mills when he turned eighteen years old. Nine months later, he went back to Florida and proposed to Grandma."

Marcus dials his mother to let her know they have arrived at the house, and he would be by in a few minutes to pick up the children.

Renee gathers up her purse and the bags they had packed for the trip to the mountains. "Sarai, we have known each other for a while, and you have never talked to us about your family."

"That's because I didn't want to deal with the memories."

"The memories don't sound so bad, hon."

"Well, there are some things I just want to forget were even a part of me. Those were joyful times hanging with my grandparents. The rest I just blocked out. A lot of hurt and a lot of pain, and I didn't realize just how much until I got that phone call. I thought I could buy some time and it would all work itself out. I am not sure which way to go, Renee."

"Is this the phone call you were talking about?"

"Yes."

"Do you want to talk about it?"

"Yes, but not right now. I just want to rest. I was not anticipating my parents coming to town. I need to put my focus on dealing with them for now. Renee, can you prepare breakfast for us in the morning?"

"Yes, and I will give them a call to make plans for ten o'clock tomorrow morning. That will give you time to sleep."

"I have a favor to ask of you, Renee."

"Sure, whatever you want."

"I need you to come with me to Montgomery for a couple of days. Is that okay, Marcus?"

"Yeah, I'll make arrangements for the kids. Mom can keep them. Renee and I will talk about it tomorrow, but that is not a problem."

Renee turns toward Sarai, placing her chin on the headrest. "Whatever you need, I will be right there with you."

There's a slight chill in the night air of June from an unexpected cold wave that has battered Georgia and Alabama residents from up north. Still dressed in standard blue attire from this morning's activities, Marcus makes a valiant effort to hold back the wind with his favorite one-button unlined blazer. As he steps down from the Navigator, he grabs Sarai's black overnight bag from the back seat. He walks over to the passenger side to open the doors for Sarai and Renee.

"Are you going to be okay, SC? You want me to help you?"

"No, Marcus, I'm fine. Stop worrying. Go ahead and we will meet you at the house."

"I am going to drop off her bag in the guest room and head on out to pick up the kids. Do you two need anything while I'm out?"

"No, can't think of anything. Sarai?"

"No." She holds on to the car door for support and climbs down slowly.

Sarai closes the door and grabs Renee's arm as they follow the elegant stone walkway toward the front door.

"I need to tell him a few things before he heads to my mother-in-law's. I will fix you and me a cup of tea and we will sit and just talk until the kids come home. By then your medicine would have kicked in and you'll sleep through the night."

"That will be great." Sarai holds on to the rail and climbs the five steps leading to the house.

Marcus rushes down the steps two at a time and grabs the keys from the antique oak hall table he and Renee picked out last year while visiting Africa.

"I'm going to take a seat in the great room, Renee, till you're ready," Sarai calls over her shoulder.

"Sounds good, Sarai."

"Renee, I checked the answering machine and her parents called. Here is the number. They want me to meet them in the morning and follow me to the house."

"That's fine. I will give them a call shortly after I get Sarai settled. I'll be back, Renee, in a couple of hours. By then she should be ready to head to bed and the kids won't disturb her. You know how they get when they see their auntie, and she will end up playing and reading with them all night."

"Good idea. I will see you in a few hours." Marcus kisses his wife and shuts the door behind him.

Renee locks up and waves from the glass partition to her husband as he backs out of the driveway. She hears the teakettle whistling in the background and thinks to herself that sleep will be delayed tonight. Renee enters the kitchen through the hallway.

"Thanks for heating up the water, darling." Renee turns down the fire and pulls two wide ceramic teacups from the cabinet. "So, what kind of tea would you like?"

"Whatever you have is fine."

"I have some Darjeeling. Is that okay?"

"Yes."

Renee rubs the back of her neck and reaches for the container. "It's been quite the day." She spoons cream in her cup and adds three cubes of sugar for her guest, the way Sarai likes it—bare and the essence of the herb, with only a hint of sweetness. Adding hot water to the brew, a pure, rich aroma invades the kitchen. She takes a seat next to her friend. The warmth of the cup, coupled with the steam from the hot liquid against her face, is calming and most appreciated. Renee takes a sip and crosses her legs, a familiar and nerve-wracking stance often demonstrated by this warrior before her attack.

Like a dog spraying his territory to signify his personal space, Renee's demeanor speaks for itself. Sarai knows she is intruding on deadly ground. Renee is not pleased with her nondisclosure attitude, especially since her life has always been an open book, which wasn't easy. Sarai knows her friend's patience is running thin, and the only remedy is to talk.

Renee pushes her cup to the middle of the table and folds her hands in the lap of her skirt. "You want to tell me what is going on?"

Sarai looks at her, afraid to utter a word. She knows she violated the girlfriend trust clause, and her privileges will be revoked soon if she is not careful. She has also learned one hundred and one street survival tactics from her, and where Renee came from, they were not opposed to raising the trunk.

"I'm waiting for an answer."

"I know you are." Sarai grabs the cup from the table and stares blankly at her own reflection dancing about in the warm black fusion. Her focus, now in the distance, tries to push its way to the front of her clouded mind. "I have put a great stress on our friendship, and I am sorry. I have not been honest or forthcoming about my life. I suppressed my past in order to survive—right or wrong, it's what I had to do. Can you understand where I'm coming from?"

"Yes, but I wish you felt comfortable enough to talk with me. You don't have to hide anything. We've been through a lot, and I am upset that you allowed things to get so bad that it could have cost you your life. But sometimes God has to take you to the edge for you to cry out."

Sarai looks at her friend like a child who has been caught stealing from the cookie jar. "Do you forgive me?"

Renee retrieves her cup and takes another sip. "How could I not?" God had taught Renee much about not trespassing upon others' seasons of life. Though the temptation to reach out prods her to dive into involvement, it isn't always right. Timing is everything with Him, and she had learned that lesson the hard way. Premature movement based on assumption could cost her everything. Planting and reaping accompany all seasons. Both require getting dirty and, more often than not, those times were private and personal depending on the method of the harvester.

Sarai puts her hands up to her mouth, clamps her lips together tightly, and thanks God for a second chance to make things right with Renee. Their friendship is as priceless as gold to her, and she needs to make good on the time and love Renee invested in their relationship. She would not take it for granted again. "I have so much that I need to tell you. How much time you got?"

Renee uncrosses her legs, letting her know a truce has been called and she has permission to enter. But her hand still rests on her lap, meaning that Sarai should proceed with caution. "All the time you need."

Sarai relaxes.

"Sarai?"

"Yes, Renee?"

"I would suggest that you start at the beginning. That's as good of a place as any."

"I grew up in the country, twenty-five miles west of Montgomery." She is relieved to have the opportunity to finally talk to someone about her life. "Our family, at the time, owned thirty acres of beautiful open land. Years later, my father acquired the remaining forty acres that sat east of our property line." She shivers as her mind travels back to times long ago. "It's getting a little chilly, Renee. Can you turn the air down?"

"Sure." Renee resets the thermostat and grabs a throw from the closet to wrap around Sarai's arms.

"Thank you."

"You're welcome."

Sarai digs deep with her body into the soft chair. "There was always something exciting happening at our estate. Twice a year Grandpa and my daddy would have freshwater blue gill flown in to fill our pond during the summer months. They entertained a lot of their business clients with fishing right on our property. We had a few horses, a lake that fed into the Montgomery River, a farm, and a five-port car house.

"The only other person that stayed at the estate was our housekeeper, Pinky. She used to babysit me on Tuesday evenings. Nayia would be at dance rehearsals and Mom would be getting ready for her bridge parties. While Mom was getting dressed, Pinky was downstairs in the pantry chewing snuff and reading the obituaries from the morning paper. Pinky searched the papers to find out who was having a wake that night, and as soon as Momma and Nayia left, she would tote me in her 1978 blue Nova across the railroad tracks. She couldn't read or write much, so I read the address she wrote in chicken scratch scribbled on a napkin.

"Sometimes, we drove for hours on back roads with red clay dust trailing behind us. We ended up in towns with only one stop sign, a five-cent store, and a jailhouse to take care of business."

"What was the so-called business, Sarai?"

"Well, Pinky and I would walk into funeral homes with Ms. Pinky dressed in black, rolls of fat protruding from her waist girdle from years of cheese grits and saltwater mullet from the Gulf of Mexico. She had a closet full of mourning wear and a comfort level with death to go along with her wardrobe. Pinky was known for her strange bedfellows. Momma said Pinky buried three husbands and had a reputation for being more slippery than an eel that didn't want to get caught. Before she crossed the border into the United States, it was rumored she was under investigation for feeding her men with more than just great sex. After they could no longer fill her ferocious sexual appetite, she sent them to an early grave with a cheap tweed suit and a quick prayer. She would stand over their unmarked graves with her shoes stretched out from being worn too often—combined with the weight of her body pressing down the sides that were now collapsed around what was left of the two-inch heels—and say, 'God bless this here soul; come running, Lord, if he belongs to you before darkness grabs a hold. Amen.' Three scoops of hard soil tossed over a body bag and a fist full of daisies were the only last will and testament before they were dipped six feet into a hole.

"Pinky was a forty-five-year-old, size twenty-six, half-Black, half–Puerto Rican immigrant who took care of her mother and nine brothers and sisters. Years later, she ended up being my saving grace. Anyway, we found funeral homes she wanted to case. Pinky and I would sit outside for a few minutes while she smoked a cigarette and listened to Tito Fuentes and Celia Cruz. That's where I got my love for Spanish jazz. Sometimes, it was the Motown flavor with a mixture of old Marvin Gaye or Smokey and the Temptation 8-tracks blasting from busted car speakers. She would take a couple of puffs, eyes half-closed from the smoke, and say, 'Sarai, I want you to give the performance of your life. *Yo quiero que tu me des el desarollo de tu vida.* Do you understand what I am saying to you, Sarai? Sarai, *entiendes lo que yo te digo?*'

"Shoot, it was fun to me! I gladly went along with her plans. 'Yes, ma'am! I understand and I can do it. *Si, señora. Yo te entiendo y yo lo puedo hacer.*' It was the only Spanish I knew. She would ask me the same question with every robbery. I would nod my head in agreement to the beat of Nina Simone.

"Pinky would smile, take a draw, and put the cigarette out in the car ashtray. She would reach over me to pull out her .45 magnum from the glove compartment and stick it in her waistband. I am so glad she never had to use it. Not sure if she would have been able to find it quick enough to get us out of trouble. We would walk into the funeral homes with white handkerchiefs up to our faces and tell the funeral director we were relatives of the deceased. She could pass for Black or Hispanic easy. If she had to speak slang, she would. If she had to speak Spanish, it was not a problem. No one paid attention to me because Blacks and Hispanics were notorious for taking in strays. My part was to cry. I would pretend I was so sad and fall out on the floor with grief. The funeral director would be busy getting me cookies and punch while Pinky would busy herself with stealing the jewelry from the dead folk's casket to support her drinking problem. She would grab me and say I was to upset to stay and she better get me home. Every time, the funeral directors would be standing there saying, 'We understand.' Pinky and I would get back in the car and examine the loot so she could estimate how much booze to buy for the weekend. She would always say, 'Best take from a dead man. Dead men don't talk and there ain't never no witnesses. Ain't gonna help them none now when they stand before the Lord, so I might as well take it for myself.' She'd stuff the jewelry down her 44DD bust and head down to the nearest pawnshop and liquor store. That's how she justified stealing.

"Pinky wouldn't dare steal from my father, though. I think she feared him more than she feared God. If my parents found out, they would have killed both of us. Ironically, she never spent most of what she took. I think she felt bad robbing those people. Many days, I would find freezer bags stuffed with ham hocks, burnt bread ends, and jewelry she had taken from her dead victims. At the end of the year, she would take what she didn't cash to the homeless shelter."

Sarai grabs a pillow from the couch and presses it against her stomach. "Now, my grandfather was my best friend and he lived down the road. When he passed, Renee, I was amazed that someone could feel that type of pulling on their heartstrings and still live. You know what I mean?"

"Yeah, Sarai, I do." Renee gets up to heat the kettle to warm up their tea, grabbing some shortbread cookies from the pantry on her way back to the table.

"Daddy said Grandpa Chameleon died of a stroke in his sleep, but I knew it was from a broken heart. I was devastated. I wanted to jump right into that casket. Anyway, he missed my grandmother terribly and he was never the same after she died. The love between those two was simply magical! My grandpa, throughout the years, courted my grandma till the day she died. He always brought her fresh flowers. I would catch them dancing to old thirty-five albums that he played on this ancient three-legged stereo player. I remember looking through the banister rails and laughing. He would say, 'I see you, Sarai, peeping in on real love. You don't know anything about this, girl!' He would wink at me and that was my permission to come downstairs and watch.

"Grandpa would come in from a day's work on a Saturday evening. He would go into the city to take care of man's business, whatever that was. That's what Grandma would call it. Never did find out what that man business was. He would come back from town always around seven p.m. Grandma would be singing in the kitchen, baking homemade bread, or breading chicken for supper. The table would be fixed up with a nice linen tablecloth, ruby-red dishes, and sparkling glassware. There was always a single candle in the middle of the table with fresh-cut flowers that he personally picked out from Uncle Shivers' back yard. Grandmother's jasmine perfume mixed with the aroma of ginger and nutmeg from her baking as she swished back and forth throughout the house, getting ready for Grandpa to come home. My little heart would be racing in anticipation for him to come through the side door off the kitchen, as though it was the first time all over again for both of us. I would hear the clock chime right at seven p.m. and at that exact time I would see the headlights from his car turning onto the gravel road that led to the side of the house.

"Grandmother would rush to the closest mirror and wipe the flour from her face, put on her red Desoto lipstick, and touch up her hair. A rush of wind is all I felt as Grandmother hurried to the door to greet him. You would hear the thin mesh screen door open and then slam. He would whisk her in his arms as if he had not seen her in months! Kiss her ever so passionately and slip his hand down the small of her back. He would arch her body gently in his arms, resting perfectly in his embrace. She was a beautiful, petite woman with Navaho Indian, German, and Black heritage. Quite a lady. And he was quite a man. I don't think I'll ever see a man so in love like my grandfather."

"Your grandfather sounds amazing!"

"He was. They were—together. Anyway, her hair was down to her waist, and it would cascade back from her neck as Grandpa removed the gold and pink hair comb shaped like a butterfly from the bun on her head. Grandma would only wear her hair down for him. The wind would be blowing in through the windows from the summer night. It would dance in through the long sheer curtains that hung in the kitchen and up the skirt of my grandmother as if someone was delicately and discretely blowing against the soft fabric, lifting it only slightly in the air. You could see only a glimpse of the rolled-up stocking fastened at her right thigh. He would lift her out of the dip and look in her eyes, stroke her hair, and ask her all about her day while dancing to scratchy music from the stereo playing in the background. A penny wrapped with scotch tape around the neck of the record player kept the album from totally being destroyed. But they were happy with the simple things in life. They were so in love!"

"My God, that is so beautiful!"

"Yeah, my grandparents were great people. I miss them. I miss them a lot. After Grandpa died, my father expanded and remodeled the house. The 8,000 square foot home with six bedrooms, nine bathrooms, maid's quarters, and a guest house grew by an additional 4,000 square feet. My father totally remodeled the estate along with my childhood history. I never liked the place after that, so it was not a loss for me when I made the decision to move to Birmingham. My grandfather did not care about notoriety or power. He just wanted our family to be healthy and happy. My father, on the other hand, lived for it like a drunk chasing the last sip from a bottle, his tongue slurping desperately for that drop that could keep the high alive.

"I remember waking up in the middle of the night one late summer evening from a loud argument my mom and dad were having about my father's tumultuous pride and temper. I climbed in the bed with my sister, seeking refuge from the loud outbursts of my mother and the neurotic pacing of my father as she followed behind him pleading. Fear could never hamper my curiosity; I was a nosy child so I would head to the door, despite my sister's warnings, and listen from the three-inch gap where the door did not quite touch the carpet. I could see the shadows of my mother walking endlessly back and forth in their bedroom. She would be shouting about how my dad was going to get this family killed if he didn't stop agitating white folks. They weren't only hanging poor Black men—the rich ones were targets, too. So often she would remind him that we were living in Alabama. It was about respect. It was not about the money anymore. Our family had more money than most prominent white families. Mom didn't understand that Dad would have given all he had earned for the respect of the white business world. Dad didn't understand the price associated with seeking approval of man.

"From the butcher block, it was a one-time non-refundable fee, and the cost was your soul. He was smart and could make the money ten times over if he wanted to. He was educated in the finest schools. My father was the only seed of my grandfather and he made sure Dad had the best education money could buy. But no matter how many degrees Robert P. Chameleon had, his skin was still black. A doctorate in business from Harvard printed on lambskin could not erase that fact. It left a bitter stain on his heart that manifested outward in every aspect of his life, including us. He was always just a needle short of being consumed by anger. He thought that one day respect would come courting and he would be ready to accept it valiantly, like a jilted, scorned lover who finally received the attention denied by his wayward pursuer. Still, he was simply a Black man from Alabama, a freak accident. That was from the rumor mill, of course, not proven data. He was not a freak of nature by a long shot.

"As a little girl, I recollect numerous wealthy Black families, but it was like trying to spread a jar of jelly across ten loaves of bread. Always, the Black dollar has been stretched too thin.

Grandmother said from the time my dad was conceived in her womb, he fought as if he were being trained for the match of the century. He kicked and turned constantly, his feet bearing down on her uterus, keeping her bedridden with pain for days at a time. She concluded he was trying to battle his way through the birthing canal prematurely. Ironically, he ended up being premature by two months.

"Dad has always been known for his grandiose entrances, and his delivery into this world was no exception. Mom would tell us our father wanted to get here as soon as possible to make right what he felt was due Mother Chameleon. Grandma, while she yet carried him in her belly, would tell my dad stories about her childhood in Florida. He would listen astutely through the umbilical cord, jotting down in his mind every word formed through the tears and every scorned emotion beating from her heart as he plotted his revenge. What else could any respectable son do than uphold the honor of his mother?

"She fed him stories of survival from the deep woods of Alabama, where cornstalks grew ten feet in height and rows of cotton surrounded copycat wood-frame houses built by fathers and their sons. Unlike my grandfather, my grandmother came from very humble beginnings . . . beginnings where your education was earned in the church that operated as a school for ten surrounding counties during the week. It ended with basic arithmetic and spelling. The goal was for you to be able to count your wages from ironing or being a dust farmer. No more, no less. A fancy education would do you no justice. Your best resources were the Bible and a good pair of knees to keep you ever present before the Lord.

"The midnight riders were the biggest threat at that time—in a single run they could burn all you had toiled and labored for in one swoop. The hooded creatures often rode in the cool of the night with torches illuminating the corn-like lanterns. They would saddle up in formations of two with the leaves whistling in the wind as they galloped through hundreds of rows of cotton patches seeking prey. Black folks became the targets of their rage because they showed up in town during election time, or they escaped their dealt hand of injustice by managing their way up north. Unfortunately, the cloaked men would come seeking the next survivor to stand in for the escapees during death's toll. The saints would say, 'In situations like this, Lord forbid when we come a-knocking there is no "do not disturb" sign hanging on your door.'

"Disturbed by the stories he heard, my father would kick out in anger. Grandmother would rub her stomach full of life to calm his spirit. She would trace her stretch marks with the tips of her fingers—lines forged from his outcries, carving out my father's destiny. She'd say, 'Son, those were times when I didn't know that the berry was bitter.' How would I have known if I hadn't tasted before? I didn't know anything else. Just hard times and Momma figured that was the plight of most Blacks. It was simply life and we made do.

"Biscuits and gravy were the norm. It tended to stick to your ribs and didn't cost much to make. Great-Gram made hers from scratch; white bread from the store was a luxury. The nearest general market was thirty miles away, so cupboards stayed full of fifty-pound bags of flour and sugar that would last throughout the winter. As children, Grandmother and her siblings would warm potatoes in the ashes of the coals, peel them and sprinkle a little salt and butter for a Sunday evening winter treat. The place of gathering was the fireplace that heated the house and served as a roaster for peanuts that had been doused in salt water. The favorite game of choice was gray horse after school. 'I got a gray horse.' 'Well, I want to ride him.' 'How many times?' If you guessed the number of shells, the prize was the peanuts.

"Love, for families, was pinnacle. Blacks may not have had two nickels to rub together, but they had one thing you couldn't put a price tag on and that was love. Folks back then celebrated life and death together. A woman stayed home for weeks after bearing a child and the elders from all around would bring gifts. A toothbrush, mouthwash, or hose was a rare and extravagant commodity to receive. In death, cooling boards were used, and the deceased were stretched out for days at a time so that mourners could view their loved ones while the farmers made the casket and headstone. Gram would say it was a strange homage long in fables and weighted in traditions out of courtesy for the grieved. White crop farmers would pass by spitting insults—calling them porch monkeys and lazy mules—but no one paid their insults any mind. Black folks felt bad for white folks dead, their own cast them away like curdled milk. They were despised and ridiculed for failing in a system that was tilted in their favor. They were a sore to the eyes and a thorn in the side, proving that their system was indeed flawed. There was no time to ponder white folk insults. Bible thumpers knew the day that person exhaled their last breath was the day the soul was required to return to the giver of life. Nevertheless, from birthing to homecomings their lives were simple yet honorable.

"As with any 'day in the life of,' there was the occasional unforgettable moment. For Gram it was the invention of the automobile. Every once in a while, a shiny new car, the color of a silver dollar with white walls fresh out of the plant, would venture down the long dirt road leading to the small farm. The community didn't consider it happenstance but divine intervention, giving their valley of trouble a river of hope that there was something much better. Yes, you could hold on for better days.

"Eventually she left Flomington, Alabama, and headed across the border toward Pensacola, Florida, to work for the paper mill. Others headed north to absorb the seductive perfume of the streets and sparkle of big city life in cities like Chicago, Kansas City, and Philadelphia. They migrated rank and file into huge factory assembly lines to push the envelope for big business during the day and to fill the pockets of organized crime during the night, their roots dug up and forgotten in exchange for the purch: watered-down liquor and cheap quick-picks from sleazy bookies. Sad to say that the unsuspecting were like deer struck by headlights, dazed and bedazzled by the glamor. It was simply too much too fast. They lost their lives to the reaper who charged a hefty fine to squat on his territory. He patrolled the alleys and gutters of the inner city and hung his accomplishments proudly from the necks of those taken down by skid row in the prime of their lives.

"Fortunately, Gram was too afraid to venture far from home. She felt safe as long as she could see red clay dirt on the soles of her shoes at the end of the day. When Gram finally had enough of nothing, the taste of something pushed her destiny. She came full circle when she married Grandpa and politely took the seat as heiress to the throne of the Chameleon Enterprise, proving that, yes, people can miss what they never had. God truly blessed her in her affliction. Royalty she was, and her sorrow became a triumph with the birth of my father.

"Her father, who is Mr. Robert P. Chameleon, is as smooth as water and as rare and rich as black sand. The one and only, the original, and there could be no second or juniors. He is from a vortex of rebel trailblazers in Black economics."

Renee's interest in the intimate details of Sarai's background is evident by the way she sits: wide-eyed, leaning forward, and chin resting in her hands. "Are you and your father close?"

"I think I will always be his little princess, but he was very hurt when I left Montgomery. I couldn't tell him why I chose to leave. He wanted me to come back home after graduate school to work. Me going off on my own tore a chasm between us, but I know I have my dad's heart, as any girl does.

"I told him I was moving to Birmingham. If silence could talk, that would have been the time to package it for distribution. I was in Europe and grateful for the distance. There would have been no way for me to tell him face to face."

"What did he say, Sarai?"

"All he said was he respected my choice to try to make it on my own. That is when I learned that sometimes there is more power in what you don't say than what you say. His silence has haunted me for the last three years. It's one of the reasons I have not been in contact with my family. I used my business as an excuse to stay away. I know my father has great respect for hard work, but I also know his love for family surpasses that. I knew I would have to sit down and explain my actions one day. I didn't want that day to come." Sarai looks over at the stove and notices from the display that it is now eleven thirty p.m. She has a full day ahead of her tomorrow.

"Where did the time go, Renee? I think we better call it a night."

Renee pushes her chair back from the table to stretch her legs. "I think we should as well. Let me give Marcus a call. He is still at his mom's. I am sure he is sound asleep on the couch in front of the television. We can get the kids ready for choir rehearsal first thing in the morning."

Renee grabs Sarai's hand. "I want us to finish the conversation tomorrow after your parents leave. Okay?"

"I never thought I would be able to tell my story. I feel like a weight has been lifted from my shoulders."

"Good!" Renee stands and stretches. "We will let tonight worry about itself. Come on, let's get you out of these clothes and into something a little more comfortable. We will have an early breakfast with the children before your parents arrive."

"Thanks for everything, Renee."

CHAPTER IV

BROKEN GLASS

"The unexamined life is not worth living."
Socrates

I t is seven forty-five a.m., and Friday night was casual and accommodating—much needed and long overdue. Renee's invite to a lazy evening was more than welcomed, and a cool Saturday morning has come too quickly after a long, hard week at work. Not to mention the unmentionable: Mr. Russell Belding, his name rolling from Sarai's tongue like a bitter herb. Hurting like a small grain caught in her tooth, the pain pulsates and rings in her ear. Her mouth is thick with fumes of anger, pasty from words she couldn't speak, leaving her jaw stained with resentment. His unexpected call is a major agitation, like fingernails across a chalkboard. Nevertheless, the jolt was needed to deal with the unthinkable, the unimaginable. Life has a way of bringing a person full circle. You can run, but you can't hide. The past can be a constant reminder that eventually you will have to face your own worst enemy—yourself.

"Hi, Auntie Sarai! Wake up. Breakfast is ready! Momma said come downstairs!"

Small, clammy hands smear across her face, waking her abruptly from sleep. The little fingers are those of her godchild, Keisha, Renee's daughter from a rendezvous with a Black prison guard during her incarceration.

Back in the day, Renee's father had a numbers runner who was a young, handsome brother from Harlem. Her dad trusted him explicitly, occasionally allowing him to drive his young daughter to school. One day, during a heavy snowstorm, she got caught with more than a little frostbite and has been nibbling on wheat toast ever since.

During her stay at the prison, abstinence was not her thing, and an officer provided a quick fix to the loneliness and monthly ups and downs of hormone changes. It was a hefty price to pay for a romp in the midnight hour. He vehemently denied to the warden that he was the father. On the record, this type of conduct was not allowed. But off the record, it was encouraged from all parties represented. Everyone was willing, kneeling, and binding to the highest bidder for extra library time, drugs, and an assortment of favors. The lowdown dirty dog claimed it could have been anyone. In fact, he serenaded her with the option of an early-term abortion since he was up for lieutenant and the scandal would cost him his promotion. She opted to have the child and he lost his job when the blood test results came back conclusive. Thank God she had the wisdom to overlook the stares from officers and fellow inmates, and the strength to press pass the ridicule. Had she not, Keisha would have been an "I wonder if" or a "what if I had" conversation that would have plagued Renee for the rest of her life. Instead, Renee is blessed with a good man who loves her child as if she were his very own, making her decision worth all the sacrifices.

Keisha pulls the covers off her aunt and plants a cold, wet, grape juice kiss on her cheek. "Auntie, Daddy said you are going to stay with us for a while. Is that true? Is that true?"

Sarai looks up to a beautiful almond-colored face with big gray eyes staring down at her. What could be better? "Just for a few days, my love, but I will make sure to set some time set aside for you and your brother so we can hang out and play games."

"That will be fun, Auntie!"

Renee enters the bedroom and sees the mustard paisley-print duvet sprawled across the foot of the bed. Her daughter, dressed in a blue polka-dot pajama set, lays nestled in the arms of Sarai. She shakes her head, suppressing her grin, and walks across the room to open a window, letting in the fresh, cool air from last night's cold front.

"What a sight! I don't know who is spoiled worse." Renee brushes the hair from her face while wiping the residue of pancake batter from her hands on a red checkered apron. "Young lady of mine, I told you not to wake up Sarai."

"It's okay, Mommy, she was already up. Weren't you, Auntie?" Keisha looks up at Sarai for confirmation.

Sarai pulls herself up, resting her back against the high arched Queen Victorian mahogany headboard. "Well, not exactly, but it was worth it to see this cute little face!" She squeezes Keisha's cheeks, and she blushes from the attention.

Renee draws back the drapes on the remaining windows and opens the blinds. "Are you feeling a little better this morning?"

Sarai attempts to move, but Keisha has settled herself into her right rib with no plans of moving unless otherwise instructed. Renee takes a seat on the side of the bed. Sarai wiggles her toes under the top sheet and rotates her head to the left and then to the right in a semicircle. She feels the bones crack and adjust under the pressure.

"Yes, the sleep helped." She looks across at the digital clock to make sure there is enough time to cover all the activities of the morning.

"Your parents called at 7:00 this morning. Marcus will meet them at the Hyatt Hotel and they will follow him back to the house. You've got about an hour to get yourself together."

Sarai yawns. "That's plenty of time. Thanks for letting me walk through some things with you last night. It made all the difference in the world. I don't think I would be able to see my parents today if I had not gotten those buried memories off my chest."

"You feel like you're ready?"

"I guess so. As ready as I am going to be. There will be no perfect time."

"You're right about that, hon. In life, there are milestones you just can't plan for, no matter how hard you try. You and I will talk later today after your parents take off for Montgomery. I made breakfast for the kids and will finish cooking when your parents arrive so everything will be fresh. Is that all right?"

"Yes, thank you."

"Coffee is on if you'd like to slip down and grab a cup. In the meantime, I would like to get into the shower while Marcus is here to watch the kids."

"Where is he, by the way?"

"Girl, please. It is Saturday morning and he's with my son downstairs watching cartoons. Come on, little girl. Let your aunt get ready."

"Oh, Mommy!"

"Let her stay for a few minutes," Sarai interjects. "I'd love to have her around, she says, while reaching her fingers toward Keisha's belly to tickle her.

"Okay, but don't be long. Your grandmother is coming around 9:30 to pick you and Meat up for choir rehearsal."

Renee closes the door and Keisha leaps up on the bed, her thick, sandy brown pigtails springing in the air. One of her favorite things to do is comb her auntie's hair. Her mother will not hear of it—not on her best day. She grabs a comb from the dresser next to the bed and begins to fix Sarai right up.

"Auntie, are you happy that your mommy is coming?"

"Yes. I have not seen her in a while."

"I would be sad, too, if I had not seen my mommy in a long time. Who would fix my cereal in the morning? Who would help me with homework?"

Sarai finds her precocious niece's reasoning soothing and refreshing. Keisha wraps her short, chubby arms around Sarai's neck for a long hug and climbs down from the bed to head for the door.

"Where are you going?"

"It's almost time for Grandma to pick up Meat and me. I will say a prayer for you today. We pray before we sing."

"I would appreciate that."

"When I pray, I am going to pray with my eyes shut really hard."

Sarai laughs. "Why with your eyes shut?"

"Because that's when God knows that I am for real about what I want, and He answers. My brother put gum in my hair while I was asleep. I was mad, so I told him when we went to church I prayed to the Lord with my eyes shut that he would get a whipping for sticking gum in my hair. I prayed, 'Lord, get him real good and, oh yeah, get him for touching my food with his nose finger!'" She looks at Sarai with her eyes wide and a cat's grin across her face. "Later that night, he got the worse whipping!" Keisha sticks out her chest with certainty that it was her prayer that did the job. "That's when I realized that for sure God answers prayers! Well, you know, Meat stopped doing that. Sometimes I pretend I am praying, and I see him standing there shaking, pulling on Momma's dress, trying to get her attention, but she doesn't pay him no mind. Momma be gone in the spirit."

Sarai laughs and is surprised by her comment. "What do you know about that?"

"A lot! It's where mommies go when they need help from the Lord. They say, 'Jesus! Jesus!' Mommies all over the church throw up their hands and start talking like babies. Then the nurses bring them tissue and water."

Sarai laughs at Keisha's naïve comments.

"Auntie, I have to tell you a secret." She looks around to make sure unwanted ears are not privy to her private conversation. "I have to be really careful, because I don't want anyone in trouble because they made me mad, and I prayed with my eyes closed."

"Keisha, you better get down these steps, little girl. Now!"

"Coming, Mommy! Auntie, can you tell me my favorite story before I have breakfast?"

"Sure, sweetie! Come sit on my lap," Sarai offers, patting her leg. "Now, how does the story go again? Let's see. Well, did you know that red was the first color perceived by mankind?"

Keisha pulls herself up onto the bed, settles in Sarai's lap, and pretends as if she is hearing the story for the first time. "No, Auntie."

"Well, I heard, while getting my hair braided as a little girl, that Momma heard from Big Momma who, by the way, was told by Great-Grandma Pearl. It was a woman who sought the color red from a long time ago. Word has it she reached her hands up through the heavens, through the rain, sleet, and snow! Finally, her hands made it and she grabbed hold of that color red, brought it back down to earth, and knitted it into a fine thin red thread. That red thread was immeasurable in strength and in time. That there woman worked till sun up—sometimes all night—till that red thread was primed. Her labor proved worthy, 'cause the next thing folk knew, that red thread was seen in the handkerchiefs of some of the greatest women that walked the earth—like the famous Sojourner Truth. For sure, Great-Grandma Pearl endured. Big Momma said she saw the red thread in the hospital gown when the doctors pronounced Grandma Pearl dead. Can you imagine? A hundred years of age before Grandma Pearl passed away, but by then that there red thread was weaved in countless numbers of women's days. Momma would say, 'Stand up, girl, and look out yonder and see.' Sure enough, in everyone that passed, that red thread was visible to me! It was in choir robes and little-girl dresses that I saw that red thread. Mothers, daughters, and churchwoman who wore fancy hats about their heads. There were nurses, wives, and teachers too. Guess what?"

"What, Auntie?"

"I went to church and that red thread was all over the pews! That there red thread linked us together as one, giving us strength to be the staircase upon which dreams are built upon. It gives us support, love, and courage to strive. Who is the source of that thread, little one?"

"Jesus Christ!"

"Yes! It was from His hem, that color red, that the woman pulled down from the sky. Amen!"

"Thank you, Auntie!"

"You're welcome, baby."

Keisha gives Sarai a big kiss and jumps down from her lap. "Will I see you after church?"

"I will be right here waiting for you."

Keisha heads downstairs for breakfast while Sarai begins to prepare for the meeting with her mother and father.

"Mommy, I'm finished eating!" Keisha holds up her small, pale blue, empty, ceramic plate.

"Let me see, little girl."

"All gone, Mommy!"

"Good girl!" Renee takes the plate for washing, unaware that the bacon and eggs from her daughter's breakfast were snuck under the table to the dog.

"Can I get down now?"

"Gram is here, Keisha!" Meat runs past, pulling his sister's hair and almost knocking her from her seat.

"I'm gonna get you!"

"Stop it, both of you! You can go, young lady. Come on, let's get your jackets. Lord, Sarai better not have kids. I'm not gonna be able to take it." Renee pulls out two small windbreakers from the hall closet.

Meat slips his arm in the small jacket with his fist clutched around some lifesavers and gum. "Are you going shopping, Mommy?"

"No. Sarai's mother will be here soon, and your father and I want to be here to meet them. Then later your father and I thought it would be nice for us to spend some time together."

"What would you and Daddy be doing without Meat and me?"

"Maybe we will go for a walk in the park, or to a movie."

"Can't Daddy afford something nicer?"

"You both are too grown up. Finish putting on your jackets. We don't want to keep your grandmother waiting."

Meat rubs his fingers through his curly red afro and picks at the frame of his wire-rimmed glasses. Meat was premature by a month. Renee had to be bedridden the last three months of her pregnancy. In spite of that, Meat still manages to give his sister a run for her money. Strong as an ox, just like his dad.

He wheezes from running up and down the corridor and grabs his inhaler. "Are we staying all night again with Grams?"

"No, you will be coming home to have dinner around seven o'clock."

"Good, because Auntie said she would be waiting here for me so we can spend some time together," Keisha interrupts.

"That's not true, Keisha. She said both of us, not just you!" Meat retaliates.

She sticks out her tongue and snatches his candy from him.

"Mommy!" Meat whines, pointing a finger at his sister.

"Stop that! Leave your little brother alone. Now, I want you and Meat to be good in church."

"Yes, ma'am," they chime in unison.

"No fighting."

"Yes, ma'am."

Keisha crosses her fingers behind her back and runs to the car. It was fine with her. She had bigger plans. Today she was going to speak to God. She figured she could get Him to take some time out of His busy day to fix her aunt's problems. After all, she knew the secret to getting a prayer answered.

Meat stomps to the car behind her, upset that his sister has made him miss sitting in the front seat again.

"Okay, children, put on your seatbelts."

"Yes, Grandma."

"Renee, I will have them back by six. What time is dinner?" she calls out the passenger window.

"Not till seven."

"Is six o'clock too late?"

"No, that is perfect, Mom. Actually, that will give me some time to finish up some cleaning around the house with the kids out of my hair. Thanks again!" she exclaims, waving them off.

"You're welcome, honey. I will see you at six."

As her mother-in-law pulls out of the driveway, Marcus pulls up with a 1993 Black 600SEC Mercedes Benz following behind him. They are a little early. Renee yells up the steps, "Sarai, your parents are here!"

"I will be right down. Give me fifteen minutes!"

Renee hears the bathroom door close and then the phone suddenly rings. "Hello."

"I'm outside, baby."

"I know. I see you. Is everything all right?"

"So far so good. They seem like nice people. They were very grateful that we were here for Sarai. I told them it could be no other way; she is family to us. Let me pull into the garage—can you let them in?"

"Yes, I'm standing at the front door now."

The driver of the expensive car emerges. A towering distinguished looking man with high cheekbones and deep-set eyes appears from behind the wheel. He is dressed in khaki pants and a loose white mesh pullover. The invisible currency of power exuberates from him like a bodyguard. He walks to the passenger side and opens the door. A beautiful five-foot-two-inch, slightly toasted-colored woman emerges in all her glamor and style. She is dressed in a simple Jackie A-line flower-patterned dress, Coco Chanel glasses, and a large, bowl-shaped, lime-green Dior china bowl-shaped hat. Perfect arm candy: the only things missing are flashing cameras and an entourage of fans. Wealth has preserved them both—they look as timeless and pricy as red-amber.

"I would have never thought her parents were fifty-two, Marcus." Renee observes Sarai's father while the phone dangles within her fingers.

"I know. They look good, don't they? I am going next door to help John out in the yard. I will find out what work-related papers I need from Sarai over dinner."

Renee is caught in a whirlwind of adoration and is mesmerized by the style and grace Sarai's mother possesses.

"Did you hear me, Renee?"

"Wow. Yeah, yeah, honey. That is fine. My word, what a handsome couple. They're coming up to the door. I'll talk to you shortly." Renee hangs up and opens the door. "Good morning, Mr. and Mrs. Chameleon. I'm Renee. It's nice to finally meet you both."

Mr. Chameleon extends his hand to greet her. "It's nice to meet you as well. We can't thank you enough for taking care of our baby."

"Trust me, your baby does a good job of taking care of herself." Renee feels the question from the unspoken lips of Mrs. Chameleon before it is proposed. "Please don't be concerned. The doctor said she will be fine. Sarai only needs a little rest. I have a young daughter of my own and I know how we worry as mothers."

"We appreciate everything you and your husband have done for her."

"It's no bother at all. Come in, please, and make yourself at home. She will be down in few minutes. May I get you a cup of coffee or some tea?"

"Robert, would you like anything, honey?"

"I would love a cup of tea with a little brandy, if you have any."

"I can accommodate that. Mrs. Chameleon, what can I get for you?"

"A cup of coffee would be just fine, dear."

"Great. We can have a seat in the family room. I am making a late breakfast for us."

"You didn't have to go to so much trouble."

"It's not a problem at all. Besides, your daughter said it's your favorite mealtime." She leads them down the hall toward the comfortably furnished room.

"You have a lovely home."

"Thank you very much, Mrs. Chameleon."

"You can call me Naomi."

Mr. Chameleon walks behind them, admiring the artwork displayed on the walls leading to the family room. "I can hear you have good taste in music. Who is the jazz fan?"

"My husband, who learned everything he knows from your daughter. Those two can sit for hours just listening to music. I assume she adopted that hunger from you?"

"Yes, and her grandfather. Nice track, Renee. Dexter Gordon, *Over Main*, recorded in Paris in 1961, right?"

"Hey, you got me on that one, Mr. Chameleon. I only know the basics, and around here lately if it's not recorded from Sesame Street, I don't have a clue. Marcus and Sarai picked up a classic from an album auction last weekend. It's the black and red album jacket to your right."

Mr. Chameleon picks up the cover. "Charlie Parker with Strings, recorded with the Royal Symphony in France, I think, in 1949. Well, well . . . impressive! Our daughter has retained a lot, Naomi."

"Yes, she has. Her grandfather would be proud."

"Feel free to look through the collection and play whatever you like. Our home is your home. Make yourselves comfortable and I will be right with you." Renee leaves them to situate themselves on the plush sectional sofa and returns to the kitchen to gather china teacups, silverware, and linen napkins from the turquoise, West Indian–style armoire given to them by Sarai as a wedding gift. *My, my . . . Mrs. Naomi Keeling Chameleon is absolutely delicious and delectable, just as her daughter described. I have heard of such women, but never seen one for myself. Just yum-yum to the tummy and quite expensive to maintain, I am sure. Hard to replace and heavily insured; high dollar in today's market. Home grown from the finest nannies, finishing schools, and advanced etiquette training passed down by the who's who of upper crust Black and white society. That is what you call platinum meow for men who can afford it. There are some who spend their lives searching for just a niblet, never mind the whole kit and caboodle. That cheddar was definitely kept wrapped and preserved in gold foil, soft to the touch, aged and bred just right, lightly scented and full of flavor. An irresistible delicacy added to a rich man's treasure chest.*

As Renee puts together a platter of assorted pastries, she remembers Sarai describing her mother's carte blanche life as a child. She grew up on an old plantation in Cairo, Georgia, where oak trees lined both sides of the driveway, curving inward to form an arch all the way to the main house. Naomi Keeling Chameleon was the eldest of the three Keeling sisters. She was born of aristocratic Black French Indian slave owners who made their wealth by importing indentured Black servants from Portugal from masters who could no longer afford to keep them during the birth of the industrial revolution. They were folk who never chewed the bitter herb of slavery. New technology made trading antiquated and very costly to maintain, but was still quite lucrative in the United States, especially in the South. Her family purchased goods and additional services four times a month from the muddy banks of Savannah, Georgia, and Jacksonville, Florida. Sarai had told Renee that the local patrons served up tales about spirits of slaves who died along the passage to the U.S. and drained the tide low, keeping the coastline dark and murky. This made it difficult for ships to dock at the port in order to sell their family members who made it across miles of sea. They drank the water, thirsty for what they were deprived of: love and life. Sarai said that as a little girl her mother always hated the water for that reason.

The Keeling family was among the few African Americans who owned Black slaves, and Naomi's grandfather took unauthorized liberties from those that he kept. One night, he didn't return home and was found beheaded in the lake that ran behind the house. When the family arrived on the scene, there was a beautiful hazelnut-colored twelve-year-old girl lying partially naked and shaking in the cold swamp foliage. A product of his appetite for the help he purchased, and the victim of his desire gone awry, and way too far. The girl told Naomi's grandmother that the souls of the slaves who died in the swamp trying to get to freedom took him. But she knew better. The child looked just like her husband. The taste of poisonous blue crow berries still hung from the grandmother's palate, baked in her bread by his jealous lover. Too much dipping caused him to fall onto the ax of his scorned lover, who said that this would be the last daughter to endure such horrors. Grandmother Keeling grew tired of looking over her shoulder for slaves whose hearts pumped with hate from being owned by a Black family. The slaves couldn't reason how someone who looked like them wouldn't understand their pain or why they would keep them in chains.

Sarai said Naomi didn't talk much about her father. They say he had the pleasantries and social decorum of the most refined gentleman but was really a bad wind that couldn't change. His name was Sir Devon Picard. Sarai found out his name from the birth certificate her mother attempted to hide in a hope chest under books of old green stamps that were collected during World

War I. Soon after she found it, that certificate vanished just as quickly as he did. Naomi made Sarai promise not to ask about him ever again. Love can be the greatest feeling and the biggest hurt. Renee gathered that he drank the milk without buying the cow, that his charm was too much, and Sarai's grandma succumbed to his advances.

Back then, the elder women believed that not shaving your legs would keep you from having sex, and routinely monitored their young daughters' limbs for the rough stubble caused by razors and lye soap. They understood allowing even a little taste in those days could cost you everything. Subsequently, Sarai's grandfather married another woman instead of Naomi's mother and disappeared into the Louisiana bayou, never to be heard from again. Some folk say he was lured by the calls from overrun swamps, seduced by a medley of voodoo, spells, and powders mixed in big pots by Creole women with skirts that dragged the muddy grounds of graveyards, women whose breasts were weighed down with chicken feet, bones, and locks of hair from their unsuspecting victims. Come to find out his mother was a witch who fell in love and married a man she called back from the grave. Love had come down on her hard and she wasn't ready to give him over to the death angel, yet she didn't want her son to grow up without a father. Satan, being the businessman that he is, was not happy about the loss of his investment, and he came a-calling one evening on a promissory note signed in blood. Naomi's mother's lover was never seen again, just his boots left on the porch pointing south. Some say the fallen one personally escorted him home to his mother. God would not have stopped him. Satan, unfortunately, had every legal right.

Naomi's grandmother vowed that would not happen to another Keeling woman. She eventually sold the house and all supporting properties and moved Naomi's mother and her other two daughters to Savannah, where they blended in with ease into the Black social scene. Enough money would bargain for the "tossed noses" to look the other way. The aristocrats would ignore the taboo; however, they may have bent heads in forgiveness but never forgot, and their sons were directed along another path. Naomi's mother was considered spoiled and unfit to be a bride and never married. Grandmother Keeling died at the ripe old age of eighty-two, and her body was shipped to Cairo to be buried in the family plot.

Naomi's mother spent the next seven years making sure her daughters moved in the right circles and that their flowers did not come into bloom until the eve of their honeymoons. She had learned from her mistakes and her daughters would not make the same error. Miss Naomi Keeling met Sarai's father at the Wimbledon tournament in 1953, when Althea Gibson was the first African American woman to play. She was introduced to Sarai's father and knew she had to have him. But in those days, a proper woman had to play it low and wait for a formal letter requesting permission to visit. Approval had to be granted by the parents. Sarai's father, Mr. Robert P. Chameleon, being one of the most eligible bachelors, was, of course, granted visitation, and courted Sarai's mother for a year. Five months later, he married Naomi in the company of some of the most famous and well-known diplomats from Georgia and Alabama. Within six months of their marriage, Naomi's mother died in a fire in the family summer house in Milan. She, as well, was returned to Cairo to be buried.

Naomi's two sisters still reside in Savannah. The middle child married old North Carolina money and currently has no children. The youngest sister remains single and adopted a child. She resides as executor over the Keeling trust; both aunts are very active in the community and local political scene. As with the rest of the family, Sarai has kept her distance over the last three years until now. Sarah, come; come, Sarah.

"Here we go!" Renee carefully presses her back against the antique white-washed swing doors and pushes through to the family room from the kitchen while balancing a tray full of over-priced baked goods and freshly preserved strawberries. She places the platter on a glass coffee table positioned between her guests, and hands Sarai's father a mint-green porcelain cup from Pakistan. The cup is etched with thin gold overlay around the brim and filled with a steaming medley of Earl Grey tea mixed with aged Hors d' Age, Armagnac brandy from France that was given to Marcus by one of his clients.

"Thank you, Renee."

"You're welcome, Mr. Chameleon. Try some of this fresh fruit." She lifts the top from a small hand-blown bowl that she made in her Friday night pottery class.

"Don't mind if I do." He reaches for a helping of polite-conversation food while she pours coffee with a hint of cayenne pepper, chocolate, and nutmeg into a large mug for Sarai's mother.

Renee plops down on her loveseat in front of the bay window, positioning her at a comfortable distance directly across from Mr. and Mrs. Chameleon. Just close enough to say, *"Mi casa es su casa,"* but also, "I am still the head Irish girl in charge, so don't get too relaxed." Propped against the black and gray marble fireplace behind her sat a 1968 Louisville Slugger baseball bat given to Renee by her dad. She was not against swinging it in conjunction with her rosary beads. Five Hail Mary's and two lumps across the head was the cure for any level of disrespect.

Renee was always on guard, often bombarded with racial insults from cackling black and white hens. "Hmm," the sisters would say, "he just needs to tap into some Texas crude, rich, dark oil. He would remember then where he comes from: between a Black woman's legs and not any powder." Over clinking wine glasses, white women would say, "Cheers, darling. I can understand her curiosity. I have tasted it myself and it was good. But marry one of them? You've got to be kidding!" Yes, it hurt. It hurt from way down. They couldn't do much about the restaurants they frequented or other events attended together; however, it would not be tolerated in her house, not from anyone.

Naomi nibbles on a plain croissant and slowly takes a sip of coffee, making sure not to burn her lips. The sweet aroma fills her nostrils. "This is an interesting blend. Where did you get it?"

"From a coffee shop downtown close to our office. It's one of my favorites. The owner imports it from Venezuela."

Naomi takes another sip and leans back, crossing her legs as she learned in finishing school: the right leg slightly elevated above the left leg, the left hip tilted at a ninety-degree angle, leveraging just a little thigh into view. A gracious position taken in front of many of Mr. Chameleon's business partners, a respectful flirtation that Mr. C adored. She was his and would not be had by another man. His confidence stood steadfast in their devotion for one another, just like the love of SC's grandpa and grandmother from her father's lineage. He gained much pleasure in showing her off, and she adored showing up and out for him.

"Renee, this coffee certainly has a kick, and yet it's tasty even without cream or sugar."

Renee smiles with great pleasure to see Naomi pleased. She knows they are a hard act to satisfy. "Yes, it is a nice blend."

"I see where Sarai gets it."

"Gets what, my love?"

Mrs. Chameleon gently wipes the corners of her mouth with a linen napkin, making sure not to rub off her burnt-orange earth-crumb lipstick. Renee looks on in amazement that she managed not to get a drop of color on the clay mug. That was a secret Renee would ask Naomi to divulge when they got to know each other a little better.

"Your daughter doesn't like cream in her coffee either, just the juice from the beet—raw and uninhibited." Renee bends forward for a handful of grapes, not sure if she crossed a road totally foreign to Sarai's mom. Slang was hardly spoken over tea and crumpets at the local country club, she was certain of that.

's eyes lock with Renee's as she sits up on the edge of the ....on and begins to laugh heartily at her response. "I understand completely, my dear! It's an acquired taste passed down through my side of the family. We are not big fans of sauces, condiments, or additives, preferring all-natural."

Renee welcomes the break from the stifling air cut by Sarai's mother's laughter and begins to feel more relaxed. "Tell you what, I will send you home with a couple of samples."

"I'd like that."

Renee drops a cube of sugar into her coffee. "How long will the two of you be in town?"

"Not long." Mr. Chameleon abruptly interrupts the women and takes the last gulp of coffee, mostly brandy left at the bottom of the cup, certainly good to the last drop. He turns toward the balcony, glancing up at the walkway overlooking the great room and begins tapping his index finger on the face of his eighteen-karat red-gold Italian Renaissance–inspired Naloni watch.

Renee homed in on the one-of-a-kind design when he extended his hand to greet her at the door. She immediately noticed the eye blinder, admiring the similarity in style to the one she'd considered purchasing for Marcus in celebration of their last wedding anniversary. Unfortunately, her paper did not extend that far—the price of that watch would have paid both of her children's college tuitions in full.

"What is holding up Sarai? I have to return to Montgomery tonight to prepare for a long meeting Monday morning."

Mrs. Chameleon places her hand on his knee and fumbles with the immaculate, heavily starched crease in his khaki pants. "I'm sure our baby will be right down, Robert."

"I'm afraid I will have to take the blame for that. My daughter, Keisha, thought it not robbery to occupy her godmother's morning, and, of course, Sarai obliged." Renee finishes off her half-eaten baguette and swallows the last corner of java from her cup.

Renee heads over to the breakfast bar to retrieve her house keys and finds them lying among a barrage of old AA batteries, coins, and ten-cent ballpoint pens tossed in a flat wicker basket. "My husband is next door helping out our neighbors and I have been summoned to assist," Renee explains from across the room. "He just called; we are having a big barbeque tonight for the families in our cul-de-sac."

"That sounds like a lovely evening among friends, darling."

"It should be. Anyway, Marcus and I are just a shout away if you need anything." Renee grabs her cell phone from the counter and pages her husband to let him know that she is on her way. She drops the device into her duffel-style carrying bag and straps it across her back. "It was my pleasure meeting you both. I am sure we will have an opportunity to talk again soon."

"Likewise, precious heart. May I use your powder room?"

"Certainly. It's around the corner and to your left. As soon as you touch the floor with your foot, it will trigger the light to come on for you."

"How ingenious! Robert, we need one of those, hon! My word, the things created for convenience!"

"Trust me, more user-friendly for our little ones than anything else. Marcus loves a gadget. That, by the way, is not always a good thing."

Naomi rises and heads toward the bathroom and stops just short of the hallway to thank Renee. "Your hospitality was most appreciated. I can see why my daughter would be drawn to you and your husband. She is very fortunate to have such good friends."

"Why, thank you. That means a lot to me."

"Absolutely." Mr. Chameleon adds a few more drops of brandy to his cup. "My sentiments are the same. Please let Marcus know he must come down to Montgomery for a visit and golf."

"I will certainly tell him. He would love that." Renee climbs the four small steps next to the kitchen that lead to the landing.

She turns and waves goodbye as she fades into the distance of Saturday's eleven o'clock shadow.

From the other end of the upper-level walkway, adjacent to the guest suite, Sarai stares down into the family room through the dark oak grid-style railing. She shifts her body weight hard into the cornflower-blue walls as if the sheetrock will absorb her fear and support her anxiety. Her toes dig deep into beige nylon-spun three-inch-thick carpet fiber, keeping her feet cool and dry. She closes her eyes while releasing a sigh. No matter how old she gets or how much experience she obtains in life, having to give an account to her parents is never easy. She can never get grown enough. She views her reflection in the large oval mirror attached to the rustic dresser in her temporary accommodations and sweeps any loose hair into a tight up-do.

"Sarai?" Renee stands at the top of the ledge with her hands folded across her chest. She looks down at her guests and back at her best friend. Always nice to have a home-court advantage. It comes in handy from time to time.

Sarai puts her hand over her heart. "Girl, you startled me." Nervous, she had secretly listened and observed her parents' conversation with Renee, hoping for signals or signs of how they might feel and what they might be thinking. Nothing from either of them: both were relaxed and as calm as two cougars. *My parents could charm the needles from a porcupine and, unbeknownst to Renee, she took the bait hook, line, and sinker. That was the infamous sting of the Chameleon lineage.*

"Well, what did they say?"

Renee puts up her index finger across her lips and shakes her head in disapproval. "This is where I draw the line. I'm not getting in the middle of you and your family. I will say that you have nice parents, and I can tell they are devoted to their own. I am sure everything will be fine. We can talk when I get back. I am going next door with Marcus. Your father is getting restless and impatient, so I would suggest you head downstairs."

Before Sarai can respond, Renee turns and heads back down the stairs. Sarai listens to the keys jingle as Renee locks the door behind her. Sarai thinks Renee missed the signs. It is the quiet before the storm; she knows they are not just here to check on how she is doing. Uncle Shivers could have delivered that message and it would have been well received by her parents. No, there is another agenda and Sarai prays that the day goes well.

CHAPTER V

HONEY & POMEGRANATES

*"All changes even the most longed for have their
melancholy: what we leave behind is part of ourselves.
We must die to one life before we can enter another."*
Antole, France

"**P**apa! Mother! It is good to see you!"

Sarai arrives downstairs to greet her parents in a puffball yellow pullover sweat top and loose rider jeans. Her face is bare, and her hair is pulled up in a ponytail twisted at the top of her head. She looks refreshed—sweet and as innocent as a little girl. Excited and pleasantly surprised at the level of ease that has come over her, she runs to embrace her mother, who has made her way back from the powder room.

"Momma!"

"Sarai, my baby!" As Naomi locks arms with her daughter, she tries not to knock over the sweat of Renee's brow from toiling in the kitchen earlier. Naomi pulls her daughter in closer until their bodies meet, hugging her long and hard. She checks for any sign of sickness, knowing she is just like her father and holds nothing

back in expression. "You look beautiful, baby! Do╒
Have you been eating right? What did the doctor s╲

Mr. Chameleon grabs his wife's waist and draws her ╲
him. "Give her time to breathe, Naomi."

"I'm just glad to see her, Robert. I am, I am! So glad to see you, sugar!"

Sarai grabs her mother's hands and places them across her heart. The coolness and familiarity are comforting. "Mommy, I am fine. Stop worrying." She turns to her father, who is fighting back tears. A simpleton could see it was a losing battle.

Lifting his reading glasses slightly, he wipes his eyes with a white handkerchief taken from his breast pocket. He attempts to clear his throat from the knot formed out of years of missing his Sarai so much. He is overwhelmed and understands intuitively he needs to be a comforter and not the disciplinarian. His face, as well, is an open book to those who know how to read him. He shakes his head and sighs.

"It has been too long. Come, my darling." He opens his arms to receive her.

Her father lavishes her with warmth and approval, which was needed and could only come from him and not her mother. She touches his face, tracing his eyes and lips with the tips of her fingers. "I have missed you so much, Papa! *Papa, je vous a manqués beaucoup. Mon l'amour pour vous ne mourra jamais nous sommes la famille pour toujours. Je suis votre fille.* [My love for you will never die. We are family forever. I am your daughter.]" She cradles his hands into hers.

He kisses her on the forehead. "*Je vous l'aime aussi, mon Sarai, et il est vrai que nous sommes la famille pour toujours, mon amour.* [I love you as well, my Sarai, and it is true we are family forever, my love.]"

When Grandfather died, my father and I stood in silence on the edge of his burial site, holding each other in disbelief, watching each shovelful of dirt as it was being dumped on his mahogany casket.

Everything about that day seemed surreal. I prayed, "Lord, let it not be true," but with every heap of clay a sliver of hope that he would return to me was lost. No, I would have to go to him. Time stood still in our grief. Not that I wanted it to. I found myself wishing it would hurry itself along and console someone else. Time and I were not friends, my heart torn by his assignment to escort my grandpa through the heavens. I made up my mind as a child back at the estate that you could not depend on such an elusive force. This was not a healthy relationship. It was full of many disappointments, nothing less than pompous circumstance due to the nature of his job and his first loyalty. He answered to the Creator, and I could not get upset about him following orders.

In the midst of light rain and thick fog, oversized dark umbrellas, and mourners dressed in black suits, my father and I made a vow: we would carry grandpa in our hearts forever. We both took Grandpa Chameleon's death very hard. I lost my best friend. My dad, well, he lost not only his father, but his rock, his mentor, his strength, and pal. After Grandpa's homecoming, Daddy channeled all of his energy toward his women, so I knew I had let him down when I left for Birmingham without his approval.

He lifts her chin with his index finger and looks long and hard into her brown eyes, searching for an answer, a clue that would give him insight into why his daughter has been away from the family, from him, for so long. After all, this was his little girl and they had made a covenant. Besides, Mr. Chameleon doted on his girls as any good father would and took it very personally that she left so abruptly with little or no explanation. Nevertheless, now was not the time for the why, why, why's or the me, me, me's. Instead, he makes sure to tuck his emotions in his back pocket, far away from her view. His weakness was the two ladies in the room and the one he left in Montgomery.

She stares back, knowing his objective was to find an answer, but today is not the day to divulge that information. Not now, not this way. She needs a little more time. Occasionally, time, her elusive friend, cooperated, and he promised to deliver on her behalf in this situation with her father.

He guides her to the couch, and they take a seat next to each other.

"Sarai."

"Yes, sir?"

He takes a deep breath and crosses his legs. "Your mother and I have talked at length since we received the phone call from your office assistant. After many discussions and prayer, we have decided that it would be best for you to come back home." He leans back and puts his arm around her shoulder.

Naomi nervously pulls a pack of smokes from her purse and taps the head of a cigarette on top of a silver compact in preparation for the battle of wills. She knows both are stubborn and these strong minds dig deep in fertile soil from Sarai's father's side of the family. She knew her daughter would not give in so easily. How could she? The lion that runs through her husband Robert's blood roars through Sarai's as well.

"Your mother and I have been patient."

"Yes, we have, Sarai." Her mother fumbles for a lighter at the bottom of her bag.

"We have sat quietly and watched you over the last few years. We have not gotten involved or tried to interfere because you have to learn and grow. That can only happen through experiences. Your mother and I were grateful that you only moved to Birmingham, so we let you work your goals. We are very proud of your progress and accomplishments, but the family feels it's time for you to move back to Montgomery."

I don't open my mouth. Choose your battles wisely, and this is not a fight I am willing to take on. I don't know a soul who has fought against my father and won. He is a determined man and gets what he wants when he wants it. I will have to be strategic in my action. Now is not the time to react; if he wanted, he could have Chameleon Enterprises shut down in a matter of days. As far as my father is concerned, this is a fancy hobby and nothing else. The family business is his priority and Nayia and I are the sole heiresses.

"We want you to move your company to Montgomery by the first of the year," Mrs. Chameleon interrupts abruptly. "Sarai, do you think Renee would mind if I took a smoke outside on her deck?"

"No, but when did you start smoking again?"

She dances past Sarai and the low-cut, Asian-inspired, contemporary coffee table, and affectionately pats her daughter on the head. "Never mind that, darling. You know I can stop whenever I want. I'll be right back."

Before Sarai can ask what was going on with her mother, her father hands her a business card with their family's attorney's information printed in bold black letters. "Call Joel next week. He will be expecting to hear from you. I decided the best way to migrate you back to Montgomery would be in phases, starting with a satellite office in downtown Montgomery. Marcus can run the Birmingham location until we can get you completely moved and staffed. There are two office complexes just west of downtown that will accommodate your needs. You can choose whichever facility you like."

Sarai's mind rushes with the how, the why, when, and where. "What about my staff, Papa? I have ten employees with families that depend on me!"

"This is a business decision. It's the cost of doing business."

"It certainly is not what I want, Papa!"

Mr. Chameleon looks at his daughter with his jaw clamped down tight. "You're coming home. If I gave you the impression that there was room for discussion, I apologize. That was a gross error on my part. You will return to Montgomery."

Sarai pulls away from her father in shock. It is too much to consume . . . first the call from Russell, now this.

Realizing he has been short with her; he attempts to change his approach. "They can and will find another job to get by. You can't save the world."

"That is not the point, Dad. These are my friends. I have built a life here. My godchildren are a big part of my life. You know how I feel about Marcus and Renee."

"They can relocate, Sarai. If not, then Marcus will have to find another career."

Sarai falls back on a medley of green, purple, and blue over-stuffed pillows, overwhelmed by the demands of her father.

"Baby, I know this is a lot for you to deal with right now, but your family needs you. I am sympathetic to how you feel about your friends, and I respect what you have built here in Birmingham, but you are needed at home. Sarai, your family needs you." Mr. Chameleon sits up and stares down at the plush cream carpet.

This is the first time Sarai can see that her father is worried, and at this very moment he seems to age twenty years.

"Baby, I don't know any other way to tell you this than to come straight out with it."

What now, Lord? Maybe I should have kept my face in the pot. Grandmother would say the pot never boils as long as you stare into it. My eyes have lifted too soon and everything seems to have come crashing around me.

"Your sister is pregnant." Without looking up, he fills his cup with room temperature brandy and drinks, staring blankly at the table.

I am certainly not about to tell my father that Russell has already called with the news of her pregnancy. That would have opened Pandora's Box; everyone knows we are not the best of friends and I do not need any additional stress from Daddy's questions on why Russell would be calling me.

"Your mother and I are both overwhelmed about your sister."

"Why?"

He wipes the sweat from his forehead with a paper napkin. The rush of rich liquor to his nervous system is too much on a warm Saturday morning. "To be quite honest, Sarai, your sister and Russell are having some problems in their marriage. Last month, your sister became ill and had to be hospitalized. She is having problems holding the fluid in her womb, but the doctor said if she would stay off her feet, she could carry the child at least six months."

"Only six months? Why?"

"The specialist said she would not carry full term because of an infection that is eating at the lining of her womb. This will be her only child. She will have to undergo a hysterectomy after the baby is delivered. The baby will be at risk if Nayia can hold the child that long in her uterus. Your mother and I are concerned because she has been very depressed, and the doctors are afraid it could possibly affect the baby."

"How many months is she, Daddy?"

"Four months. Your mother and I did not find out about the pregnancy until last month. I think she was contemplating an abortion, but because of her faith she couldn't go through with it. Apparently, she is carrying the baby in her hips like your grandmother. Nayia has not put on much weight at all, but I knew something was wrong because she withdrew from the family.

"She had come to the house for your mother's routine eight a.m. breakfast soirée with the ladies from the country club, but she was sick to her stomach from the time she walked through the door. Pinky nursed her until late that evening and we decided that she needed to stay the night and called Russell to let him know. They spoke briefly. There was a polite nod and a quiet yes from your sister as she hung up the phone. I found that very odd but didn't want to push her with questions.

"Friday night we got a call from Russell that he had to rush her to the hospital and that's when she told us. I think she was considering leaving Russell. Sarai, it's possible that he was or is having an affair. I'm not surprised. His grandfather was a male whore."

"Daddy!"

"Well, it's the truth. Having no diplomacy was his calling card when it came to where he laid his hat at night. His son turned out to be just like him, so consequently Russell sucked from the same blade of grass. The boy didn't have a chance, Sarai. The icing on the cake was Pinky's comment that he had his feet under someone else's table. We haven't discussed any of this with your sister. The family just wants her to get stronger and we will deal with Russell later."

Mr. Chameleon gets up, leaving Sarai alone on the couch, and walks toward the stone fireplace. His eyes lock on the portrait hanging high above the mantle. It's an Edgar Degas original called "Blue Dancers." Sarai loves his artwork, which is considered progressive, influenced by Japanese woodblock called Ukiyo-e. Sarai and her grandmother would go through books of nineteenth-century artists and get lost for hours at a time in watercolors and strong acrylic strokes of still life and self-portraits.

"This is a beautiful portrait, Sarai. No doubt a gift from you?"

Sarai turns toward the picture. "Yes, I purchased it for Keisha last year."

He rests his hands behind his back as he turns toward the sound of a small river bird that has landed on the base of the window ledge. "Darling, it's the simple things that make life so grand. God did not design life to be so complicated for man. Sometimes we are blinded by our own inadequacies—stumbling and tripping trying to find our way. Without the Lord we cannot stay on that path, and so a lie becomes your truth. You know it but don't care until everything comes crashing down on you.

"This marriage, this pregnancy, has taken a toll on your sister's body and mind. The doctors have been watching her vital signs very carefully. I'm more concerned about the depression since . . ."

His voice trails off as he returns to the sofa and takes his seat next to Sarai.

"Since what, Daddy?"

"Your mother didn't want me to tell you, but your grandmother didn't die in a fire in Milan. She killed herself from years of battling depression over the loss of her lover. She never got over him and he never got over her. Years later, your mother's family found out that he sent many letters to your grandmother, but a Keeling could never marry a comely man. They were bred for no such thing.

"One weekend in September, your grandmother left for Louisiana to find her lover. What she found was a skeleton-framed, stoned-faced mulatto woman with ice-blue eyes, five feet tall with wild, fern-like silver hair draping to the floor of her shanty-style flat, off gator alley in the backwoods of Baton Rouge. It cost your gram a pretty penny and miles of traveling bad roads to find her. Rosa Picard, mother of Sir Devon Picard.

"Years ago, she was a high priestess to Satan, and the demons that gave her power took her youth by the time she was thirty. She proved to the towns folk, that witchcraft is a fast road to absolute destruction. It was no way to live, despite the odds, despite the poverty, it's best to have a friend named Jesus. Her nails were long and crusted black from mixing potions, her lips turned downward in an awful frown, while her voice cracked from years of chanting.

"Rosa was not happy to see the young lady who'd captured her son's heart. In fact, she tried to negotiate a trade with the minister of righteousness, but he knew this one was hands off and he had no ground to work a deal, even though he was willing. In anger, Rosa put a spell on your grandmother and sent unclean spirits to torment her day and night.

"As with most Christians, we have a surface relationship with the Lord, and she didn't know the power she had to fight them back. Between raising Naomi and her sister on her own and without a good name, the battle with depression drove her insane.

What she thought should have gone to Naomi went to someone else and she never got over it. Anyway, spirits good and bad can be passed down and I don't want to lose your sister, so I'm taking every precaution. We have every prayer warrior fasting and on their knees on her behalf. She is doing better and right now we have her in therapy. That means that you will need to come home. Sarai, I need you, baby. Your mother and I feel it's for the best for everyone."

"You put a lot on my plate, Daddy. I don't mean to sound selfish, but I don't want to talk about this right now."

"I'll tell you what. I will let you think about how you want to handle moving back to Montgomery and we can finish this discussion next weekend. I am hosting a dinner party at the house to announce your sister's pregnancy. We want you to be there for support. I will send the car for you. I'm sure there are things you need to take care of at the office, so when can you come down?"

"I had already made up my mind to drive to Montgomery with Renee. I can leave Thursday morning. If it's not too much of an inconvenience, Renee will accompany me for the weekend."

"That would be wonderful. It will give her time to check out the area and look at some property. Your mother and I will have the driver pick the two of you up at, say, nine o'clock that morning?"

"That is fine, Daddy, but you are making a lot of presumptions. I don't know if Marcus and Renee will want to move to Montgomery."

Mr. Chameleon ignores his daughter's comments and checks his watch again. "Well, I think your mother and I better head on out. We promised Shivers we would come by to see him and Ms. Oxley."

"When are you leaving for Montgomery?"

"Right after I see your uncle."

"Okay, I will call you later tonight and we can go over the details. Tell my sister I'm praying for her."

Sarai's mother returns to the family room as Robert and Sarai get up from the couch. "Is everything all right in here?"

"Yes, Mom, everything is fine. Let me walk you guys to the car." Sarai hugs her parents and directs them to the front door. "Be careful and kiss Uncle Shivers for me. Let him know I put the check in the mail. He will understand what you're talking about."

"We will certainly do that."

Sarai opens the door.

"Honey, go ahead to the car and I will be right there."

"Okay, Robert." Mrs. Chameleon kisses her daughter on the cheek. "Bye, baby. Call me tonight."

"Yes, Mom."

Sarai's father walks down the small landing and turns to his daughter.

"What is wrong?"

"Nothing, I just want you to know I am so glad you're coming home. Even if it is just for the weekend. I know you could have turned down my request. You're not a little girl anymore. I'm aware that I can be controlling. Your sister really misses you. We all do. You two were very close and it hasn't been the same for her. You and Nayia need to work out your differences. Even if your differences happen to be Russell. I knew all along that you didn't think he was good enough for your sister, but it was her choice, and you have to respect that."

Sarai drops her head. *If you only knew.*

"It wasn't your decision, Sarai."

She reaches up to give him a kiss on the forehead. *Not worth the conversation.* "'Bye, Momma!" Her mother waves back from the car. "Daddy, are you going to be okay finding your way back to the highway?"

"Yes, I will be fine."

She watches as her father puts the car in reverse and pulls out of the driveway. Suddenly Sarai feels the ache tugging once more at her heart. This time she will not be foolish by closing her ears to the harkening of its warning. This time she shall listen.

❦

Sarai hears the sliding back door open and close. A few moments later she hears the rubber soles of jogging shoes hit the hardwood floors and keys sliding across the family room glass couch table.

"Sarai, where are you?"

She yells back. "I'm upstairs!"

Renee heads up the few flights of steps to find her friend sitting cross-legged in the middle of the guest room, stripped down to a sleeveless white T-shirt and lemon-colored shorts. She is sorting through what seems like an endless pile of legal documents from her briefcase. "Hi, sweetie. We saw your parents pull off a few minutes ago. Marcus and I were thinking about you the entire time. How did it go?"

"Trust me, hon, you don't want to know."

Renee grabs a white cotton towel out of the laundry basket and runs it across the back of her neck. "Whew, it is hot out there, girl. Anyway, I can just about guess. They want you to move back to Montgomery, right?"

"Yes, and they want me there by the first of the year. That's a little sooner than I was thinking, but I knew it was coming."

Renee takes a seat on the bed and grabs a handful of children's clothes to fold. "The question is, what do you want to do?"

"I don't want to go back to Montgomery, that's for sure. But my dad is much older now and he needs some help with the family business. This is the first time, Renee, I could see age on my parents' bodies, and quite frankly it scares me. It never crosses your mind that your parents won't live forever. I have to sort it all and I want to make a decision tonight. There is so much at stake, and I don't want anyone to be hurt." In aggravation, Sarai slaps several business envelopes against the carpet. "What about you and Marcus?" Sarai stops and holds her hands to her mouth and sighs. "What about the kids? I can't leave my babies."

Renee grabs a fistful of sport socks. "I'm not sure, but it's your life, so start making some choices that will benefit you. What will make you happy? Stop living for someone else. You worry so much about everyone else getting hurt, but to your own detriment. In the long run we all pay for your compromises. You're not benefiting anyone by not standing up for what is right for you. Marcus and I will be fine. It's not like we will be miles away. At best it will take us an hour or so to get to you by car. Hey, your boy may want to follow you to Montgomery. He loves you deep, Sarai, you know that. The only problem I see is his mother, but we will cross that bridge when we get to it. Just relax, girl. You will make the right move at the right time, my dear."

Sarai closes her briefcase. "I'm getting nowhere with this paperwork. My mind is not geared up for office work." She gets up to lie across the bed, grabbing a pillow to stuff under her chin.

"We told you to leave the contracts for Marcus and Jackie. Just relax."

"Renee?"

"Yes, darling?"

"I told my parents we would be there Thursday. Is that okay with you?"

"Sure. Marcus's mother will watch the children and Jackie is more than able to handle the office by herself." Renee tosses the last ball of socks into the clothes basket and reaches across her friend to grab the phone from the receiver. She stops when she notices a small tattoo on the upper right corner of Sarai's back. "Hey what is that?"

"What?" Sarai turns toward where her friend is pointing on her flesh.

"On your back. I could barely make it out, but it's a brown chameleon. I never noticed that before! When in the world did you get a tattoo?"

"Years ago, when I was still in high school. I forget it's there most of the time. I had it done by Pinky's niece during the Cinco de Mayo festival when I was fifteen."

Renee rubs her finger across the pattern. "Funny—I wouldn't think you were the type."

"Well, it's not as edgy as getting my tongue pierced like you, Miss Renee, but it was a major milestone and symbolized my independence. Yes, my freedom, my liberation." Sarai sits up on the edge of the bed, grabbing hold of the sheets with her fist. "Now it's just a hard reminder of scars I lived through. Sometimes, I catch its reflection in a mirror when I'm getting dressed and I'm overwhelmed that, unlike this chameleon, I am unable to blend into life when things get hard or when I just don't want to play anymore. It's like trying to rub a stain from the mirror, but no matter what you do or how hard you wipe, that stain remains."

Renee sorts through a small basket of carpet and air fresheners. She shoves the small plastic container toward the foot of the bed. "I can finish cleaning later." She grabs a pillow from behind Sarai and presses it into her stomach. "Leaders don't blend well into the backdrop. God never intended for you to be a wallflower; it's the reason you don't fade well into the scenery." Renee wiggles her red toes, crudely painted by her daughter. "What is it that you want to forget so badly anyway? Is this about the phone call?"

"Yes," Sarai answers plainly.

"So why don't you start where you left off last night?"

Sarai looks over at Renee, then at the alarm clock on the bedside table. "What time are the kids due back?"

"Mom won't have them back here till six and it's only one, so we have the rest of the afternoon. Marcus is next door watching basketball, so you know we won't see him anytime soon. The steaks are defrosted, seasoned, and marinating in the refrigerator. The vegetables are all cut up and ready for the grill." Renee positions herself comfortably at the foot of the bed for a long discussion.

Today she would get her answers no matter how long it takes. "I am listening, Sarai."

"Well, I guess a lot of this struggle relates to my sister. Growing up on the estate, my sibling and I had the typical big sister/little sister relationship. I looked up to her and wanted everything she had, and she was upset because I was the baby. Nayia figured I got away with murder. I did, of course. Hindsight is twenty-twenty and I can reflectively say I was the annoying child everyone flipped their nose at, and rightfully so. It's amazing that we can sit in our own vomit and not realize that it stinks. I felt like everything that took place around our home was my business just as much as it was my parents'. My source of enlightenment, fortunately, was Pinky. She warned me that one day I was going to hear something I didn't want caught up in my ear, and it would take a long time for that sting to wear off.

"It came years later when I heard Nayia jumping for joy about the news of my move to Birmingham. My dad and mother may have been disappointed, but she sent me packing with her favorite red shoes and a smile. Nayia figured it was a small ransom to pay for me to be out of her hair. From that day forth, those shoes hurt worse than any designer flaw—a pinch that has lasted. When I wore them, they tore open the same hurt and that moment became my reality once more.

"I was grieved that she didn't mind me departing, but for her, at last, she had Mom and Dad to herself. Being the eldest, she figured enough time had been doted on little Sarai and it was her time to shine.

"Nayia was an alluring young woman, Renee, with a rose-gold-colored complexion. Smooth as mink, dainty as a pearl, with an hourglass figure just like Momma. She was my mother's protégé and mother spent much money and time making sure my sister would follow successfully in her footsteps. Nayia did her part by spending many years learning how to play the piano and learning to speak French fluently. She was representing not only the best of the Chameleon side of the family but the Keeling family as well. During the summer, she traveled abroad and went to the same finishing schools as royalty.

"For me, the downside of growing up at the Chameleon estate was that I didn't have many friends. I did have one companion: Julie Elizabeth Russell. She would come to see me when my parents played bridge with her parents twice a month. They belonged to the same country club. She was the only friend that my family would allow me to spend time with away from our home. We would hang out for hours in her mom's oversized closet full of ostrich feather wraps, long ball gowns, and stone broaches.

"Julie had two brothers. One lived in New York and the other had just left for college but would come home for the summer. I met him and immediately had the biggest crush on Mr. Light, Tall, and Bright. He had green eyes and sandy brown hair, one dimple, and a paper-thin mustache. Oh, I thought he was so fine, girl! He had a smile that was to die for and a laugh as smooth as silk.

"He was the youngest brother to Mr. Edward Belding, a very powerful voice in local politics. If you were running for any office in Alabama, you needed to shake hands with him first. He could get you where you needed and in front of the right people. Their family migrated from the West, building the Belding name by chasing tumbleweeds and beating their chests from Nevada to California. They shouted from the pulpits of soap crates, lobbying for fair wages and descent working conditions for Blacks and Asians who worked laying railroad tracks in the desert heat. The Beldings were strong centers of influence up and down the western shoreline. They raised millions of dollars for some of the most influential Black political mantras of the twenty-first century. Unfortunately, they also gained and earned a risqué reputation for spending, drinking, and much pillow talk. Daddy said they were free people that migrated from the Canadian mountains down to Washington State and were known for kissing cousins, thinking this would be the way to keep the family bloodline rich and pure. Most of the upper crust handled them with a twelve-inch stick and kept their children at bay, thinking that could be a potential stew of the worse kindred.

"Many exclusive doors were closed to that family until the late 1950s. Edward Belding was a fine man, and his father was a man of standards and integrity, hardworking and loyal. The grandfather spent his entire life rebuilding the family name. My father has had a working relationship with Mr. Belding for many years. Dad said he liked a man that let you know what direction he was coming from—that way you didn't have to guess. He was honest about a dollar and only expected what he earned. Daddy says you have to respect a man for that.

"As a young girl, I thought Julie's brother was the best thing to grace the world since the discovery of chocolate. I liked his occasional compliments when I would visit Julie. He would tell me that I was growing up quickly. That I was going to be a beautiful woman. It meant a lot since so much attention was always spent on my sister about her looks. He would always say, 'You're going to be a heartbreaker, Sarai!' I was flattered because all the big girls wanted to date him. My sister and her friends said he was 'it,' and they spent many hours out of their day in front of the mirror getting dolled up just for the chance that he would ask one of them out. Here I was, little Sarai, thirteen, getting his attention. If they only knew, I would think to myself, they would be so jealous!

"I was invited to a slumber party at the Belding estate for Julie's fourteenth birthday. Everyone who was anybody was going to be there, and I marked the days off on my calendar with great anticipation. Her father pulled out all the stops to ensure we were going to have the best time. Mrs. Belding's interest was in making sure the right parents would talk about the party months later. It was all about, 'Did you hear?' and, 'Did you see?' and, 'Money is no option.' We didn't care. We were young and it was a good time at our parents' expense.

"That day, we had our first facials and pedicures. Julie's brother, Russell, made sure his sister had all the latest music and that the maid prepared or had catered every imaginable food you could eat. However, I had my own agenda that was not listed on the invite. I wanted to see her brother and I knew he would be in town on school break. It was a calculated risk that cost me everything. I picked out my best dress to wear and I had Pinky hot curl my hair in what seemed to be hundreds of spirals. The girls played games and talked about first kisses, mostly imagined. I found it all quite boring. I had bigger aspirations than boys who were trying to fight their way through early puberty.

"While Julie opened her presents, I headed toward the kitchen for a soda. When I closed the refrigerator door, there he was! My heart raced. I didn't know what to do or what to say. It was now nine o'clock and I had on my yellow quilted housecoat and long white acetate pajamas. Hardly Cinderella anymore; that time had come and gone. He asked me about school and what I was doing for the rest of my summer vacation. I felt so important that he was paying attention to me. He admired my purple amethyst bracelet and escorted me back to the lower level of the house with the rest of the girls. They all fussed and awed over how cool he was. The girls and I talked for a couple of hours and retired at one in the morning.

"I remember lying on the sofa thinking about how nice it would be to date a real man, not some little boy who was still struggling with hormone changes and who got a boner if the wind blew too hard. I was embarrassed for them standing there trying to be cool while their weasels hammered against their jeans, excited over young girls who no longer wore training bras, whose flatlands had turned into small anthills by the end of the summer. I found them annoying, but Julie's brother was exciting and adventurous. I had no idea what adventure was, I just found the possibility exciting. I imagined dancing with him in the moonlight and under the stars. I decided then to leave my charm bracelet that he admired tucked between the cushions of the couch so that I could have an excuse to come back and see him the next day.

"The following morning, my mom went shopping with friends and I asked her to drop me off at Julie's for a visit. I would call Pinky to pick me up in a couple of hours for dinner with the family. When I called Julie's house, her brother told me she'd left with their mother, but she would be there by the time I arrived. When I got there she had not returned, so he asked me if I wanted to wait for her. I said yes and waved goodbye to my mom. He invited me to watch television in the family room.

"At first, everything was fine. He reached in his pocket and pulled out my bracelet. 'Our housekeeper found this when she was cleaning this morning.' 'Oh, it must have fallen off last night as I slept.' I reached over to take it from him, but he pulled back with a sinister grin. 'What will you give me for it?' I was startled and had no reply. I knew I had gotten myself into a mess and there was nowhere for me to run. He dangled the purple rocks in front of me like fish bait. 'Sarai, what will you give me for it?' I stuttered, 'I don't have anything.' 'Sure you do!'

"When I went to reach for it, he kissed me. It was so sudden and unexpected. Before I knew it, he had grabbed my face and was forcing his mouth hard against mine, pressing his tongue in my mouth as I tried to scream for help. All I could think about was that I brought this situation on myself. I felt such an overwhelming amount of guilt and fear. The weight of his body against mine was a force I could not reckon with, and I knew I was in trouble. He was broad and stout from playing sports and I was pinned under his frame. I looked around for any sign of help and the only witnesses were Lucy and Ricky Ricardo from an old Christmas episode. They seemed to be laughing at my bad judgment of character. Before I knew it, he had slipped me down on the couch and was on top of me, with his left hand around my neck to stabilize his body. I could hardly breathe, and I understood he was in control and that he was capable of hurting me. He snatched off my panties, dragging them down my legs. I fought by trying to squeeze my thighs together, but he was too strong. He dropped them to the floor, and I could feel the heat of his hand slipping into my bra. He moaned when he fondled my breast. I screamed as his cold tongue slithered across my nipples. He bit into my flesh and I gasped, only to taste the salt of his hand that was now pressing against my lips, smothering me into silence. I clutched at the pillows, dragging my nails across the fabric. I tried swinging my arm in the wind, rearing back to gain force as I nailed punches against his back.

"It seemed ineffective, and I was growing tired. I felt his right hand slide up my thigh and I heard the rattling of his belt as he pulled at his zipper. I could feel him pushing against me. I closed my eyes, seeing small white and blue dotes dancing in the darkness. He clamped my hands together and whispered in my ear, 'If you scream, I will kill you.' He removed his hand from my mouth slowly. I was shaking and trembling. My eyes were wide in horror. How could he do this to me? I wanted to speak, but terror had taken a seat on my vocal cords. 'This is what you wanted. I see how you look at me. Flirting and showing off for my attention. Well, you have my attention, and this is what big girls do.' He pressed my right leg to my chest. I could feel thick liquid running down my thigh. Not once did he take his eyes off me. I knew he wanted to instill terror, and it worked. 'You like it, baby? I know you do.'

"Finally, I could feel him inside of me and I thought this was the beginning of the end of my life. Where could I go? How could I show my face? Humiliation and shame rested on my soul. His groans still echo in my ear. His black skin is ever present before my eyes. The smell of his body is thick in my memory; the coldness of his sweat as it dripped against my naked, shattered body is something I shall never forget.

"After he finished, he told me to go to the bathroom and clean myself up. I grabbed my clothes and ran, locking the door behind me. I slid to the floor, sickened, and confused. I didn't know what to clean up. How could I wash away what was done to me with water? How could I bathe away the trauma I just endured? I looked down and saw lots of blood on the floor. I grabbed a roll of toilet tissue and began to make a pad. I had not started my period, but I knew what a sanitary napkin looked like. I had to get out of there quickly.

"I started getting dressed when I heard a knock at the door. 'Sarai, you have been in there long enough. Unlock this door.' I sat there, unable to move or speak. 'You either open this door or I will break it down.' I unlocked the door and stood there, afraid to make a sound. I didn't know what he would do to me. Anybody that was capable of this could do anything, as far as I was concerned. He just stood there staring. Not an expression on his face. I guess he was trying to figure out if I would tell.

"I heard walking upstairs and bags being put down on a table. 'Son, we're home!' He turned to where the voice was coming from. 'Okay, Mom. I'll be up to help you in a minute.' I tried to get around him, but he grabbed me by my shoulder, locking me into position where I stood. 'If you say one word, if you shed one tear, if you give my parents any idea that there is something wrong, I will kill you, Sarai. Do you understand me?' I believed him and nodded my head in agreement.

"That day would be the performance of my life. I did exactly as told. I didn't want anyone in my household to be suspicious, so I called Pinky at the scheduled time for her to pick me up. That was the hardest pill to swallow. Sitting there pretending everything was okay with my body aching and riddled with terror.

"Pinky pulled up at exactly four o'clock and I hurried to the car, not looking behind me. 'Bye, Sarai!' He stood there with his mother, father, and sister as if nothing ever happened and waved me away into despair. I didn't know what to do. I slipped into the car, carefully aware of what had just taken place between my legs. I closed the car door and put on my seatbelt, trying desperately not to move or turn. I pretended to admire whatever was taking place outside, so I didn't have to look at Pinky. The pain on my face would be a dead giveaway and she would beat me till she got an answer. She felt like I was her own and I knew her .45 caliber was loaded and tucked in the glove compartment. She would kill him if I told her what happened. 'Did you have a good time?' 'It was okay.' 'Well, it's me and you tonight, kid. Your mother and father are going out and your sister is staying at a friend's house.' I was relieved. I needed to get myself together. I just stared at the flat view and prayed that we arrived home quickly.

"Pinky must have puffed on an entire pack of cigarettes before we made it to the house, pretending that she didn't know something was wrong. At the time, I did not realize she had seen the bruising on my bare legs. She picked up on my troubles like a dog picks up on a scent. I knew she could sense it, but I sure wasn't telling. 'You sure you all right kid?' 'Yes.' 'I cooked your favorite—fried chicken and sweet corn. I even baked my girl a chocolate cake.' 'Thank you, Pinky.' I just wanted the day to end.

"Pinky let me out at the front door while she parked the car. I ran to my bedroom, stripping off my clothes. I drew the hottest bath that I could sit in. I must have sat there for hours, crying. When I got out of the tub, Pinky was sitting on the bed waiting for me. She had my soiled clothes in her hands. 'I would like to think that you started your monthly, but I have a feeling that's not the case.' I fell into her arms and cried. I told her what happened, and she cried. I begged her not to tell my parents and I begged her not to do anything. I didn't want her to go to jail. I knew if my father found out there would be no turning back. She grabbed my face and kissed me on the forehead. 'For now, little one, it will stay between us.' As soon as she said it, I knew he would have to pay. Pinky would make sure he got what she figured he deserved.

"Hours passed and the bleeding would not stop, so she drove me over the railroad tracks to see one of her friends. I was examined on a table in the back of a ten-cent storefront. Her friend was a short, balding Hispanic man from her country that she trusted implicitly. They spoke about me in Spanish, but I could read the sadness in her eyes. When her head dropped, I knew I was in a bad situation.

"She left my side for a few minutes. She came back with a fifth of vodka and told me to drink it. The doctor had to sew me up where tissue had been ripped. When we got home, I threw up. I cried all night and slept till late the next morning. Pinky and I put it aside. The two of us would bare this cross together. She saved my life. Pinky told my mother that I started my cycle, and she bought the story, no questions asked.

"A couple of nights later I heard my sister talking to her girlfriends about what had happened to Julie's brother. He had been mugged and beaten very badly and was hospitalized. He was in a coma. It was the talk of the town and made the news. It was his just desert administered by Pinky's cousins. She never spoke of it, and I didn't ask. I knew justice was served.

"To this day, I never told her that I continued to see my victimizer. I went back to him many times over the years. By the time I was seventeen and preparing to leave for college, I had developed so much scar tissue that the doctor said I could not have children. I again headed across the tracks to see Pinky's people."

Renee's jaw dropped. "Sarai, why? Why did you go back? What in God's name were you thinking?"

"I wasn't thinking at all. It was easier for me to deal with a relationship, no matter how dysfunctional it was, than to deal with being raped. Anything but that, Renee. At the time, if I had let that come to life in my heart, I would have died. That is how I coped. It took its toll on me, though.

"Over the years, I began to court many demonic forces. I put on my finest silk scarves and pearls and scurried off to knock on the door of depression. It answered and became my confidant. It would come to me in the middle of the night and wrap itself around me to console my pain. It pitied my groans and encouraged me to drive deeper into despair. Grief and misery supped with me often, and loneliness called out to me in the middle of the night. They held the door open for suicide and constantly seduced me with a way out. They would speak to me, telling me how they understood and how no one should have to go through such heartache; they could all end it with a slit of my wrist or some pills. I entertained the thought many times but could not bring myself to do it. I knew it was the Lord keeping me. I guess Satan figured he would have to take another route.

"About a year later, I would smell the scent of maple syrup and it was the spirit of gluttony enticing me to overeat to cover up my sorrow. I gained over fifty pounds and grew weaker. I knew that something was going to have to change. I was given a way out.

"It was the year of my graduation and I looked forward to going to school in Europe. It was the time I needed. I knew being away from him and my family would be a tremendous consolation. I left in the fall and would write him often. Not once did he reply. After a while, the letters were sent back 'return to sender.' There was no sense in worrying about it, being a thousand miles away, so I busied myself with school. It was for the best. I knew the relationship was wrong.

"About a year later, I was preparing for class when a package of assorted candies, tea, and newspaper clippings from the *Montgomery Chronicle* arrived by courier from my family. There on the front page was Julie's—my best friend from childhood's—brother, Russell Belding. The article described his family's political career and his nomination as the first African American for Alabama to be unanimously elected to the Senate. I was returning to Montgomery for Christmas break and read about the big party that was going to be given in his honor. In fact, my father's company was hosting it! I knew everything about us was wrong, but I was still drawn toward him.

"I thought I would surprise my family and show up a few days early. What I really wanted was to see him. Maybe he had changed. Maybe this time when he tells me how sorry he is for what he did, I will feel like he means it. Maybe, just maybe, this was all a bad dream. But then I would wake up.

"By the time I arrived at the Montgomery Center, the dinner had started. My plane was late and the weather was horrible. My driver dropped me off in front of the building, and when I entered the banquet hall my father was giving a speech. I stood at the back of the room as an onlooker admiring my father. He was smiling, which was something I had not seen in years. After Grandpa died, it seemed that he died as well. He looked so happy all dressed up in his black tuxedo. At the end of the speech, he introduced the honoree and shook his hand. He received a standing ovation and took the microphone. He thanked his supporters and began to talk about a woman that had been in his corner. She had encouraged him to fulfill his dreams to be the youngest Black man from the State of Alabama to be elected to the House. Her support and love moved him to his destiny. I was getting sick to my stomach. How could he? After everything he put me through. He then turned to my father and asked for my sister Nayia's hand in marriage. 'Nayia, will you marry me?'"

"Sarai, no!" Renee gasps at Sarai's announcement.

"Their engagement played out in front of the world while my life spun out of control in private. Yes, Russell Belding, my childhood friend's brother, the man who raped me, had the audacity to ask for my sister's hand in marriage. He is the reason I left Montgomery. When I heard his voice over the phone, every emotion I had penned up over the years that I buried and that I let lay dormant came down on me like a flood."

Renee tries to hide how she feels but is unable to contain her sorrow. She places her head across Sarai's back and weeps. There are no words, just uncontrollable wailing, and an ocean of tears.

CHAPTER VI

RECONCILIATION

*"It is not the going out of port but the coming
in that determines the success of the voyage."*
Henry Beecher Ward

Sarai awakens to the sound of the phone ringing in her ear. She picks up, but the caller hangs up before she can speak. She raises her head toward the window. It is still daylight. The red light from the answering machine indicator is flashing four fifteen p.m. Her mouth feels like it is full of cotton and her eyes are glazed with a thick film of mucus blurring her view. She digs for a face towel in the mix of the small pile of clothes still left on the bed.

"My head is killing me!" She hits the button on the answering machine.

"Hey, what are you ladies up to? I will be home shortly. Just called to see if the steaks are ready for the grill, baby! John just started the fire, and I will give it about fifteen minutes to cool down. See you in a few."

Sarai feels a weight on her back as she tries to sit up. It grumbles and she realizes it is Renee. She has fallen sleep with her head dug into Sarai's back.

"Renee, wake up. It's late. Marcus just called and said he will be home in fifteen minutes. Renee! Wake up."

"What time is it?"

"Four twenty p.m."

"I feel like I have been hit by a ton of bricks." Renee sits up, looks around the room, and tries to gather her thoughts. "The house is still quiet. Good. The kids are not here. I am so glad I asked Mom to bring them back late."

She reaches over to Sarai and strokes her hair. "Are you okay, sweetie?"

"Yeah, I'm fine."

"You know you hit me with a bombshell. I wasn't ready for what you told me. I am so sorry, Sarai. What are you going to do? What do you want to do?"

"I don't know yet, but we are still going to Montgomery on Thursday morning. We will have to let the Lord guide our steps. I tried to work it out on my own. Now I am going to give it to Him to handle."

"I agree."

"One thing I don't want you to do, Renee, is tell Marcus. I want to talk to him about it myself. Will you do that for me?"

"Sure. I think you should be the one to tell him." Renee hears the garage door opening.

"Baby, where are you? The grill is all set and ready for the meats!"

Renee yells back from her bedroom, "We will be right down! Dinner will be ready by five thirty. Call Mom and tell her to bring my kids home." Renee turns to Sarai. "You sure you're going to be okay?"

"Renee, this is the first time in a long time that I feel like everything in going to be fine."

❦

Thursday morning: 8:45 a.m.

The air is thick and wet from the early morning dew. It is eerily quiet for a workday. The only sound is of Marcus dragging heavy designer luggage across the hallway floor, luggage that he had stacked neatly at the bottom of the stairs before retiring to bed yesterday evening. He gathers the last few items and heads toward the front door.

"Renee and Sarai, you two need to hurry up. Your ride will be here in ten minutes!"

"We are on our way now, sweetie!"

"Women. They are so slow," he grumbles to himself. The car pulls up on schedule and Marcus heads out to place the baggage in the car.

Renee knocks on Sarai's bedroom door. "Sarai, are you ready? The driver just pulled up."

Sarai appears in a long, soft-blue, summer-sleeved cotton dress with a matching patterned wrap.

"You look lovely."

"Thank you. Did Marcus get the bags?"

"Yes. Everything is probably in the car by now, so let's go. We don't want to be late."

They exit the house as Marcus is putting the last bag in the trunk. "I want you both to be careful. Call me when you get to your family's home."

"I will, Marcus, and thank you for helping out while I'm away. I owe you."

"Yes, you do, Sarai, and you'll pay, trust me." He smiles and gives her a big hug. "It's going to be fine, and you and I will spend some time together when you get back."

"You promise?"

"I promise." Marcus turns to his wife. "Okay, baby, I have the kids for today and Mom will pick them up in the morning."

"What are you guys going to do all day?"

"I have to go into the office for a few hours, and then Meat has soccer practice, so we will be busy." He kisses his wife goodbye. "Don't worry about us. Just take care of our girl. Call me as soon as you get there."

"I will, Marcus."

Sarai and Renee slip into the plush black leather seats and the driver closes the door behind them. Sarai waves from the window as they pull off and head toward Interstate 85.

⤜∞⤏

12:05 p.m.

The gray limousine pulls onto a long, narrow dirt road marked by two narrow trees at the entrances and nothing else.

"Where are we going, Sarai?"

Before she can answer, Renee turns to see four large and beautiful brown horses racing back and forth over several acres of land. Beads of light bounce against their sleek coats from the sun that has nowhere to hide in the vast space. The land leading to the main house is massive, and there are hundreds of feet of white fencing lining the open green pasture, thick as carpet. She watches in awe at the magnitude of the property.

There was no way Renee can describe what she is viewing with her own eyes. The Chameleon Estate is a sight to behold. Its grandeur is wrapped into rows of flourishing green trees neatly lined along the borders of the main house and guest facilities. Cascading mounds of colorful flowers and exotic plants are placed as far as the eye can see. The main quarters are made of pallid stone with large white pillars that run the length of the house to support the plantation-style porch. The driver pulls around the circular cobblestone driveway to let the girls out in front of the house.

"Mother!"

"Sarai, darling!" Sarai and Renee are greeted by Mrs. Chameleon, who is dressed in silvery silk lounge pants with a purple overcoat swinging in the wind as she walks down the front landing. She hugs her daughter. "How was your trip, precious?"

"It was fine. You look wonderful, Momma."

"Thank you, my love. You know I try."

Renee extends her hand to Mrs. Chameleon. "It's good to see you again, Mrs. Chameleon."

"You as well, Renee, but remember, you can call me Naomi, sweetheart."

"Yes, ma'am. I will try to remember."

"Where is Dad?"

"At the office. I am expecting him in a couple of hours. He has already called to check on you. We will give him a call shortly to let him know you made it in. He will be very pleased that you two made it here safe. Andrea, can you take their bags to Sarai's bedroom? Renee will be staying in the guest room next to hers."

"Yes, ma'am, right away."

"Not much has changed, baby. You will find everything as you left it. Your father wouldn't let me touch a thing in your room."

"Is Nayia here?"

"No, she's at home. Doctor's orders. She wants you to give her a call about meeting her for dinner tonight. I think she wants a little personal time with her sister." Naomi puts her arm around Renee. "Don't worry about us, Sarai. We can find plenty to get into. You don't mind, do you, sweetheart?"

"No, not at all. That's why we are here, so whatever Sarai wants is fine with me."

"Good. Then it's settled. Tell you what, Renee. I will call my real estate agent so you can start looking at some properties. Andrea can drive you over to your sister's later this evening."

"Sounds like a plan, Mom."

"Yes, that is fine, Naomi."

The women head toward the front door. "I can make a phone call to have the listing e-mailed to you tonight. We can select the ones you want to view. How does that sound, my dear?"

"That's awesome!"

"Great. We have an office down the hall and to the right of where you will be staying. Come, let's get you two settled in your rooms. Sarai will give you a tour of the estate."

She grabs her mother's lounge coat. "Mother, where is Russell?"

"Your father sent him out of town for a meeting. He will be back in time for the dinner on Saturday."

"Does he know that I'm in town?"

"I'm sure your sister told him."

"What about Pinky? Where is she?"

"She took the morning off to take her mother shopping. I already called her to let her know you would be here no later than lunch time. She is so excited about you being here, darling. She has talked about you for the last two weeks. Her baby!"

"I can't believe she still calls me that."

"She will be by later today."

They enter the main hallway of the house, lined with large hand-painted pictures of the Chameleon family. Huge vases carved from rare crystal are overflowing with large red roses and sit at the foot of the staircase.

"There is still so much work to be done for the party on Saturday. Your father and I will meet you for brunch later on the lanai. Is that okay?"

"That is fine, Mother."

Sarai and Renee head up the steps with Mrs. C to unpack, but they are interrupted by the driver. "Pardon me, ladies, Mrs. Chameleon."

"Yes, Andrea?"

"There is a Mr. Wallace here to see Mr. Chameleon. He said he has an appointment."

"Oh, yes. Please let him in. I forgot he was coming by this morning."

Sarai places her purse on the step near the railing and heads back down. "Who is Mr. Wallace, Mother?"

"He was a friend of your grandfather's." She grabs her daughter's hand. "Come, Sarai. I want you to meet him. Excuse us for just a moment, Renee. You can have a seat in the great room. We will only be a moment."

They find their guest standing on the porch admiring the view with his back to the house and his hands stuck in the pockets of his perfectly pressed jean overalls. "Mr. Wallace."

He turns to see the silhouette of the two lovely ladies standing at the door. "It's good to see you! Naomi, how are you?"

"Just fine, just fine, Mr. Wallace. Robert told me you would be here this morning. He had to go to the office and apologizes that he couldn't be here."

"Not a problem at all. It's been a long time since I been down this way. It's amazing what you and your husband did with this land. Your father-in-law would be proud! Honestly, never thought I'd live to see a Black man own anything' like this. We white folks thought we was supposed to have it all. Well, God bless yah fo' puttin' your best foot forward. I remember when it was run over with old' wheat stock and peanut crops."

"Well, Robert and I are simply delighted that you took us up on our offer. How's your wife, sir?"

"A little under the weather, but doing all right for an old timer."

"That is good to hear, Mr. Wallace. Lord, where are my manners? Come on in, please. Can we get you anything?"

"No, I'm fine."

"You didn't get lost trying to find the house, did you?"

"No, not at all.

"This, by the way, is my youngest daughter, Sarai."

"How do you do, sir?"

"Well, aren't you beautiful! She favors Red."

"You knew my grandmother?"

"Yes, I knew your grandfather and grandmother. Your grandpa and I used to be porters for the same rail company. We faced many adversities being friends at a time where segregation was still strong, even up north. Did you say your name was Sarai?"

"Yes, sir."

"You were pregnant with her, Naomi, the last time I saw you and Robert."

"Yes, I was."

"Now, you're not going to believe this, young lady, but I used to rent land from a fella up north in Michigan named Dodson. He had a daughter named Sarai as well. Funny. I thought that was a peculiar way of saying Sarah. Come to find out it's not an uncommon name at all. Well, fancy that, you just never know. It's a small world."

"Yes sir, a small world indeed."

"Mr. Wallace is going to use the five acres behind the barn near the pond to graze some livestock he inherited from his brother."

"Just till I can get on my feet, Naomi. I don't want to be a bother."

"You take your time. Grandpa Chameleon would not have had it any other way. Just let Robert or me know what you need. We haven't been back there in years."

"Thank you so much. I'll come back by in the morning to take a look. Just wanted to stop in to say hello. Take care, and it was nice meeting you, Sarai."

"You as well, sir."

They watch as Mr. Wallace returns to his old green 85 Ford pickup, and waves goodbye.

"He is a nice man, Mom."

"Yes, he and your grandpa go way back, baby. Seeing him brings back a lot of memories. Always remember the importance of true friendships, baby. You can't put a price tag on them, and they are a rare commodity from the Lord."

"Yes, ma'am."

❦

1:00 p.m.

"Brunch was fantastic, Naomi! It's so beautiful out here, I don't think I would ever want dinner served anyplace else if I could have this view every day."

"We are glad you enjoyed it, but it gets real cold in the evening when this Spanish tile chills the lanai like a refrigerator after the sun sets."

"The food was delicious, Mother, but I can tell it wasn't Pinky's."

"Raven is our new cook. She specializes in Creole cuisine. That's what you taste. We hired her, what, two years ago, Robert?"

"Yes, I think it has been two years. Time flies. We hired her to help Pinky out. She had to cut back on her hours to take care of her mother. By the way, she will come by in the morning to see you instead. She is running late."

The maid enters the patio. "Sarai, you have a call. It's your sister."

Sarai scoots her chair back from the table. "If you'll excuse me, I will take the call in the hall."

She picks up the receiver. "Hello?"

"Hello, Sarai. How are you?"

"Fine, Nayia. How are you, beautiful?"

Nayia grabs her stomach, rubbing the warm life of an eight-month-old. "A little tired, but I'm doing okay. This baby keeps me up. She is a fighter, just like our dad. The doctors said they want me to stay off my feet, so I am even more tired because I can't do much. You know how we Chameleon women are: we have to be busy doing something. It's the standing still that is driving me crazy. I'm glad you made it for the dinner party. It was time for us to see each other." Both women are silent. "It's so good to hear your voice, Sarai. I have missed you."

"I missed you, too."

"I want to see you right away. Can you come over now?"

"I don't see why not. We just finished eating. I would love that, sis. Momma said she would entertain my friend Renee."

"How does she like the house?"

"A bit overwhelming for her."

"Heck, Sarai, it is still overwhelming for us."

"Let me talk to Renee and I will have the driver bring me to you."

"Great. I will see you shortly."

Sarai returns to her family.

"We were just about to have some coffee. Would you like some, dear?"

"No, Mom, I'll pass."

"Is your sister okay?"

"Yes, she is fine. She wants me to come over now. Renee, will you be okay by yourself?"

"Yeah, girl, go ahead. Your mother and I can find plenty to do around here!"

"Okay. Don't wait up for me. I am sure it will be a long night, since we have not seen each other in a while."

CHAPTER VII

REDEMPTION

*"I do not like the woman who squanders life for fame.
Give me the woman who living makes a name."*
Martial

Sarai arrives at the Belding's brownstone townhouse in the Country Club of the South. Very posh, very exclusive—so exclusive you must be invited in to be a resident. Sarai walks up four fiery burnt-orange marble steps to a large stained-glass door and rings the bell. Nayia opens the door.

Sarai thinks to herself, *She is even more beautiful pregnant, if that is at all possible.*

"Come in!" says Nayia. She moves out of the way to allow her sister to pass by and waves to the driver. She hurries to close the door behind Sarai and hugs her sister in a warm embrace. The hushed silence speaks on her behalf as they cling to one another.

"I have missed you so much. How are you? Let me look at you, Sarai. You are all grown up and simply gorgeous, like Grandmother Chameleon. You know, you favor Daddy's side of the family, SC."

"Stop fussing over me, Nayia. You're just like Momma."

Nayia places her hands on her hips.

"It hasn't been that long."

"Three years isn't long to you, child?"

Sarai laughs and grabs her sister to hug her longer and harder. She doesn't want the moment to end. "Let's have a seat, we have a lot to talk about. The townhouse is beautiful."

"Thanks. It took a while to decorate it. Since we entertain a lot of Russell's clients and his family's friends, I wanted it to be just right. Mom helped."

"I can tell. It certainly has her flair, but it has Nayia all over the décor." She helps her sister sit down in a chair that she can easily get out of and chooses a seat next to her on the matching ottoman. Sarai takes her hand. "Tell me how you feel."

"Fine," she answers simply. Stretching back, she rests her shoulders against the cushion of the large overstuffed chair.

"You look tired, Nayia."

"Just a little worried about the baby. I haven't been able to keep food down. The doctors said I have lost weight. I have an appointment next week to see my obstetrician, and if I haven't gained any weight, she is going to have me hospitalized for her sake."

"For *her* sake? What are you talking about? You already know what you're having?"

"Yes, it's a girl. Mom and Dad didn't mention that to you?"

"No. Congratulations, sweetie. Are you happy about the pregnancy?"

Nayia sits up and puts her head down. Muffled sobs begin to fall from her mouth.

Sarai lifts her head. "Why are you crying?"

"Sarai, I am in so much trouble I don't know what to do. I can't talk to our parents about this."

"Don't cry, Nayia. What happened?"

"My marriage is in shambles. It has been an uphill battle from the day I said 'I do' to this man. I found out about a year ago that

Russell was having an affair. For about the first two months of our marriage he made sure that he was here by six so we could have dinner together and talk. We spent lots of time with the families, his and ours, Sarai. Everything was going okay. Then after a while he would come home later and later, and sometimes not until the wee hours of the morning. He would say it was work related, meetings or documents that had to get out for deadlines. But I would smell perfume on him when he would lie next to me. At first, I thought I was probably imagining things, but I would get phone calls during the day and they would hang up. I tried calling back, but it was always a number I could not trace. I would question him about where he was and why he was spending so much time away from the house. He would say that he was at appointments. I didn't want to tell Daddy, and his father would lie about his whereabouts. I would ask Russell if he was seeing someone, but he denied it. After he spent last Christmas away from me and the family, I hired a private investigator. Help me up, Sarai."

Nayia gets up to retrieve a wood box carved with African art. The box was large enough to hold letters. "Here, take a look."

Sarai takes the box, hesitant to open it. She gets a bad feeling from way down on the inside. Sarai feels an uncontrollable need to run away with everything in her soul, away from this house, away from this situation. Her hands begin to shake, and she begins to sweat. *Lord, what is it?*

"What is in this box, Nayia?"

She takes a seat in the chair and stares out of the window, leaving her sister's question unanswered. "Just open the box."

Sarai opens the box. At first it looks like pictures of a man kissing his companion, but upon closer examination . . .

"Oh my God! Lord, no!"

In the box are dozens of explicit pictures of a man having sex with a young woman. As she sorts through the pictures, she can see that the women are not the same. Sarai knows the man is

Russell. Her stomach is caught in her throat as her hand rattles the box and distorts the figures engaged in various poses. As Sarai sorts through the black and white shots, she comes to a picture of a young woman straddled across Russell's nude body with her backside to the camera. Sarai is frozen in horror.

Nayia turns to her sister. "The investigator told me he found out Russell has been having affairs with young women for years. He has a fancy for younger women. Over the years, his father has paid off a lot of families for his involvement with their daughters.

"Two years ago, he got in a lot of trouble for raping a young woman from Huntsville. She was only thirteen and her family found her beaten up pretty bad when they got to the hospital. He said it was consensual and that she told him she was eighteen. A lot of hush money was paid out, and part of the deal was that she and her family would move as far west as possible.

"I didn't tell Mom or Dad. It would have killed them. His career would have folded, the family name would be in jeopardy. I was under so much pressure. What could I do, Sarai? Russell begged me not to tell and told me he would stop. He did for a while, according to the investigator, but now he is seeing someone else right here in Montgomery. I haven't said anything to him yet. It's been eating me up inside. My doctor said I have to be very careful because I could lose the baby. I have tried to push it to the back of my mind.

"I was going to leave when I first found out about the rape, but I got pregnant and thought maybe this would turn him around. He got worse. Russell is out of control, and I don't know how to stop him before someone gets seriously hurt. Sarai, what should I do? I need your help."

The room spins around Sarai, and darkness blankets her eyes. She holds on to her chest tightly, breathing erratically. Sarai bolts up, dropping her blue wrap. "Where is your bathroom?"

"What?"

"Where is the damn bathroom, Nayia?"

"Straight down the hall. What is wrong with you?"

Sarai leaps up and runs to the end of the hall in search of the door that leads to the bathroom. She flings the door open and begins to throw up violently into the toilet.

Nayia is behind, calling after her, "What is it?"

Sarai stands up and walks to the sink. She turns on the cold water to wash her face. She drops the crumpled picture on the corner of the counter. Nayia grabs it. She looks long and hard and notices the figure of the young woman in the picture. She moves toward the vanity light and then looks at the shoulder of her sister. The tattoo on the shoulder of the young woman in the picture is the same as the tattoo of the Chameleon on Sarai's back. Nayia drops the picture and screams.

"Is this you, Sarai?"

Sarai looks up in the mirror, her breathing rough and cracked. She desperately tries to form the word to tell her sister what happened years ago. "Nayia, I was just a kid! I tried to get away from him, but he raped me, I swear! Things got way out of hand, and we had a relationship, but it was nothing like you are probably thinking. I tried to break if off. I can explain why I stayed so long. I knew I had to keep this a secret. I had no idea you were seeing him when I left for school. I thought I would die when you accepted his marriage proposal. I didn't want you to marry the bastard, but I was so scared to tell you, so scared to tell Daddy. I feared for our very lives. When I got back from Europe you were already engaged. You were already in love. That's why I left Montgomery. Nayia, please believe me. I didn't mean for this to happen!"

The room begins to spin around Naia. She turns to walk out of the bathroom, tracing her hands along the wall, hugging it as she drags her body across the smooth surface, knocking down pictures. She cuts her hands on the nails that were placed to hold up the heavy frames. "This can't be happening to me. You are my sister. This is my husband. I am carrying his child."

Sarai runs behind her, trying to get her to listen. "Nayia, please talk to me!"

"My life has been one lie after another. What will Momma think? What will Daddy do?" Her foot catches the carpet, and she stumbles down the steps leading to the living room. She hits her head against the glass coffee table, knocking herself out cold.

"Nayia, answer me! Nayia!" With blood all over her hands, Sarai dials for an ambulance.

Mr. and Mrs. Chameleon rush through the hospital emergency doors and see Sarai sitting in the emergency room waiting on the doctor. They rush to their daughter.

"Sarai? What happened?"

"She fell, Mom. She hit her head really bad on a glass table."

"Where is the doctor?"

"He will be back in a minute." Sarai nervously looks at her parents. "I think they are going to take the baby." Sarai looks up to see Renee walking up the hallway toward her.

Without Sarai having to say a word, Renee knows what went down. Neither sister will be a winner in this situation, and it will take a lot of time to heal. Now is not the time—she needs her family more than her friend. Renee backs away to let her be with her loved ones. "Sarai, I will be downstairs in the cafeteria. Call my cell phone if you need me."

"Thanks, hon." *These are the types of relationships that every woman needs,* Sarai thinks. *A friend who can feel your needs and your desires without you uttering a word.*

Fifteen minutes pass and the doctor comes out from seeing Nayia. Doctor Simms is a college buddy of Sarai and Nayia's father. "She has been stabilized. Robert, Naomi, sorry we have to see each other under these conditions."

"Is she going to be okay, Paul?"

"Robert, I don't know any other way to tell you this than to tell you the truth. Nayia is very sick. She has been under a lot of stress. Your daughter has been binging and purging for at least a year. After she got pregnant, she never stopped. I told her and Russell when the reports came back that they needed to get her some psychological help. The purging has weakened her immune system and it is possible that she could have a stroke if she goes through with the pregnancy. Robert, Naomi . . . she could die. You all need to talk as a family. It's up to her, but I can't guarantee that she or the baby will make it."

"Can we see her?"

"Yes, but she wants to see Sarai first. Go ahead, hon. She is in room 535. You have ten minutes. I don't want to tire her out."

Sarai walks down the long corridor and takes a deep breath before entering the room. Her sister is strapped to an IV and several monitors. Nayia looks up.

"Come here, Sarai." She extends her hand to her little sister.

"Nayia."

"Hush, let me talk. I'm so sorry that he did that to you, baby."

"Please don't be mad at me, Nayia." Sarai drops her head into Nayia's lap, inhaling sobs between breaths.

Nayia strokes her hair. "How could I be upset with you? How would you have known? I wish I could take all of this back. Look at me, precious. I'm tired, sweetie. I'm not going to make it."

"What are you talking about?"

"Listen to me. Grandma Keeling came to see me a couple of nights ago. I told her I wanted to go with her. She said the baby will be fine. Sarai, it's my choice. I want you to go to the house and get all the papers and pictures I have locked up in the safe. Here is the combination. Also, I want you to call this guy." She tries reaching for her bag.

"Let me get it for you."

"This is the investigator I hired. Call him, and then I want you to call my personal attorney—not Dad's—and have paperwork drawn up stating that I have given you power of attorney over my estate and over the baby. I want you to name her Olivia after Grandma Keeling. She lost so much for the sake of the family, and I think it would be the right the thing to do. Plus, it would make Mom very happy, and Daddy as well. Besides, you will give Daddy lots of babies with names from his side of the family." Nayia tries to comfort her sister. "What is wrong, Sarai?"

"I can never have children of my own. When Russell raped me, it created so much scar tissue that the doctors said I could never conceive."

Nayia looks toward heaven and closes her eyes as warm tears stream down her face and into the pillow. "It will be okay, Sarai."

The nurse comes in to check on her vital signs.

"Give us a few more minutes, please."

"Sure, Mrs. Belding."

"Russell will never go for your proposal, Nayia."

"If he gives you any problems, tell him that you have information about his affairs and the case that his father paid off for him raping a thirteen-year-old in Huntsville. If he doesn't sign the papers, you will take the information to the press. This case never went to public ears. I want you to take care of all the paperwork today before he returns to Montgomery. I am sure Daddy already called him and he will be taking the first flight back. Don't cry, Sarai, it's going to be fine. With God, it is never over.

"I accepted Jesus Christ as my Lord and savior and I have peace with where I am going. I have seen our family! We have a beautiful legacy in heaven waiting on us, Sarai. I want to go home, and more than anything I want you to have what Russell took from you. This child will be yours."

"He will fight this, Nayia."

"Let him fight. You're strong and you will win. He has a lot of blood on his hands that he is accountable for. Let it be so. You will have the victory." Nayia kisses her on both cheeks.

SHE WORE THE NAME

The doctor returns. "Sarai, you need to go now. Your parents want to see her and then she needs to rest. Have you made up your mind, Nayia?"

The sisters look at each other and nod. "Yes, sir. I am having the baby and my sister and I are confident that everything shall be fine."

Sarai walks toward the waiting room and dials Renee. "Renee?"

"Yes, SC?"

"I need you to meet me in the main lobby."

"I'll be right there."

Sarai and Renee rush to file the paperwork and head to a courier to make arrangements for the letter to be delivered to Russell in the morning. They head back to the hospital in silence. The driver pulls up to a red light.

"Renee?"

"Yes, SC?"

"My grandmother on Mom's side came to see Nayia." A sparrow sits at the base of the red light, and at that moment she feels her sister passing. She grabs Renee's hand. "When we get back to the hospital she will have gone home." Sarai closes her eyes and opens them. "No more tears, Renee." She looks at her friend. The ache is gone.

Saturday morning: 9:30 am

The heat of the Alabama sun doesn't seem to warm her up. Who could have foreseen this turn of events? She certainly would not have imagined coming to Montgomery to bury her sister. Sarai walks from the gravesite with her family, including her extended family, Pinky and Renee. They are greeted by mourners extending their love and condolences. When she looks up in the crowd, she sees a familiar gray salt and pepper afro in its midst.

"Renee, is that Mr. Ross?"

Renee leans forward past the thick cluster of people in black and gray suits. "It sure is. Well, praise God! Mr. Ross! Over here!"

Sarai grabs him and they exchange smiles and hugs. "Hi, SC. I got here as soon as I could. I am so sorry to hear about your sister."

"Thank you for coming."

"I thought I would surprise you, SC."

"You did, and I am so glad you came to Montgomery, Mr. Ross!"

He hugs her. "I got the message from Jackie about your sister's untimely departure. The folks at church wanted me to let you know they are praying for you, and they are looking forward to seeing at church when you return."

"Thank you so much for taking the time to drive down here on such short notice. You don't have any idea how much it means to me that you came."

"It's the least I could do. Is your family doing all right?"

"As well as can be expected. My mom is taking it the hardest. Nayia had the same spirit and zeal for life as my mom. But she will heal in time."

"Listen, darling, before I forget, your secretary asked me to drop off these cards to you. She said they would cheer you up."

"Only Jackie would remember that when I'm sad colorful cards cheer me up. I will call her later and thank her personally."

"She said to tell you to look at the card wrapped in suede with blue ribbons. That one in particular would do the job, but she sent strict instructions that you are not to open that card without giving her a call first."

Sarai laughs and shuffles through a few cards to the envelope from her supporters. She smiles. *God's grace and mercy amidst a storm is always a wonder, and a needed touch to know he is listening and cares.*

"When are you headed back to Birmingham, Mr. Ross?"

"In a few days. I want to make sure you and the baby are strong enough first. I want to take back a good praise report to the pastor."

"Let me walk you to your car."

"I'd like that. Where did your parents go? I'd like to meet them."

"They are over by that oak tree talking to the bishop."

He puts his arms around her and opens the car door.

"Let me introduce you to them, Mr. Ross."

"No, you just take a seat and look through those cards. I will introduce myself." He moves around the door, shuffling her into the cushioned leather backseat.

She sticks her head out of the car. "Can you stay for dinner?"

"I sure can, SC. I can stay as long as you need me. I'll be right back. You just relax."

Mr. Ross heads over to meet her parents, and Sarai begins to sift through the dozen or so condolence cards when a small sheet of crumbled wax paper falls out from between them onto her lap.

> *But he knows the way that I take-when*
> *he has tested me, I will come forth as gold.*
> (Job 23:10)

She closes her eyes and thanks the Lord. *If it were not for you, I would not have been able to make it through.* Now she understands the passage of the scripture. Suddenly, like a flood, she is overtaken by a presence of evil. She opens her eyes. A shadow hovers over the car, looming above her. Russell stands before her in a black suit with an envelope balled up in his fist. He swings the door of the car open before she has a chance to lock it.

"You're not going to get away with this!"

She stares back at him and speaks in a calm, steady voice. "You don't want to make a scene now, do you, Russell?"

"There is no way I am signing this bull. I will never give you my daughter!"

"I tell you what, Russell. I will give you until tomorrow morning to think about it."

"Wait. You, making demands on me? You have to be joking. Who the—"

"Watch your mouth. People are looking at you, Mr. Belding. By the way, Russell"—she reaches into her briefcase and pulls out a folder with copies of the pictures and the court documentation of the lawsuit for the rape of the thirteen-year-old girl—"my attorney will be by in the morning for you to sign the paperwork, and when Olivia—"

"Olivia?"

"Yes, Olivia. When she gets out of the hospital, she is going with me. I expect you to make the announcement to the press. Either you do it or I will. It will probably go over much better for your family if you do it and not me."

Russell stands up and straightens his suit and tie. The storm raging in his stomach must be tamed. For now. "Mark my words, it does not end here, Sarai."

"Goodbye, Russell." She swiftly closes the heavy limo door and takes a deep breath. She remembers when she was a little girl and she and her grandfather would get up early in the morning while the dew was still moist on the blades of grass. She would put on her favorite blue jeans with a red bandana tied around her head to keep her hair from frizzing up from the moisture in the air. Grandpa and Sarai would make sure not to disturb Grandma Chameleon as they headed out the side mesh door leading to one of the many apple trees planted on the estate. Every Sunday morning, they would rise to pick fresh apples for Gram's famous preserves that she prepared for the October festival every year. Fresh apples, walnuts, nutmeg, cinnamon, brown sugar, raisins, butter, and a little honey was her recipe for success; she used the tasty combination for pie filling and turnovers. Grandpa would let her pick the apples from the ground, and she would fill up her apron as he shook the tree to allow the fruit to fall to the ground. As always, her eyes were bigger than her hands and she would try to carry too much. She would cry out, "Help me, Grandpa, help me!" He would look down at her and say, "Little girl, why are you flapping your hands and screaming for help in shallow water? You don't need Grandpa's help. God would not ask you to carry more than you can handle. Now, put some of that back till you have an amount to carry. I think that is about eight apples, right?"

"Yes, sir!"

"The same count every time. Now let's head back to the house before Red wakes up."

Sarai would never forget those words. God will only help us with the things we cannot handle. Too often we cry out from shallow water, but the deep call on the deep. Yes, He has equipped us to handle every situation He has designed personally for us. *This too, Lord, shall all work out for my good and for your glory.* She opens her eyes and pulls a compact from her purse. As she looks in the mirror, she can see Russell still standing in the road. His fist is balled so his knuckles have no color. His tie twisted and the first two buttons open on his shirt. Funny, she could not recall him ever not having everything in control. She can see his lips quivering and repeating, "It is not over," as he stares off into space.

"Driver, can you take me to our home now?"

"Yes mam, of course."

"Thank you. I will meet my parents and family there for coffee."

"Certainly, Miss Chameleon." They pull off in the black limousine, leaving Russell standing in the background near a curve, watching Sarai with an angry face. Sarai is terrified and understands she is in the fight of her life with Russell over the baby.

The driver makes a right turn on to US Route 238. He is just a few miles from some of the most prolific civil rights sights in all of Alabama. He paces his speed and heads toward Highway 65.

The driver's cell phone rings.

"Hello, this is Red Eye."

"Are you in route?"

"Yes sir, we are headed to her family estate right now."

"Is the line secure, Mr. Red Eye?"

Red Eye reaches for a smoke from his blue jean duffel bag as he is speaking to the caller.

"Yes sir, it is."

Sarai notices that he has grabbed a cigarette and gives him a glaring look, as if he were a pig rolling in sludge.

"Excuse me, can you not smoke sir?"

"I apologize, ma'am."

Much to his chagrin, he discards the cigarette into his duffel bag and tells her she has a call coming through in a few moments.

Just today, unexpectantly, Red Eye was pulled off a particularly important assignment to protect Sarai. He had been given some information on her and understood he had to ride this donkey blindly.

It was a matter of convenience for the federal government. Red Eye was in the area. Red Eye absolutely hates this type of assignment. He happened to be working in the field very closely with an Alabama secret service unit on offenses regarding the KKK for a local favorite politician and was pulled to work with Sarai. He did not expect to be with Sarai long. What he needed was a smoke, a double shot of bourbon, and the warmth of a woman, not some overindulged wealthy young female who obviously got in bed with a Jekyll, which was his own conclusion. She doesn't seem so innocent to him after reading her case and the profile on her sister.

"Who is the phone call coming from, driver?" asks Sarai.

"It is not for me to say, ma'am," Red Eye replies impassively. He puts his finger up and asks her to hold for just a moment.

That dizzy feeling in her abdomen strikes her once again and she starts to pray inwardly while she waits to take over the call.

"Yes, I understand sir," says Red Eye as he listens astutely to the caller. He mumbles under his breath in frustration, "This is not starting off right. This is not starting off right at all."

The voice on the other end of the phone says, "There has been a change in plan?"

"What would you like me to do? She has requested that I drive her to her family home. We should be there shortly, sir."

"That is two exits off of I-65 South, and I know exactly where that facility is located."

Sarai is clueless as to what the driver is talking about, and in her mind, she will not be going any other place with this man, only to her family home. There will be no pit stops for her.

"Is the witness secured?"

"She is."

"Can you put the witness on the line?"

Red Eye prepares to give the phone over to Sarai.

"Sorry sir, please hold while I get Sarai prepared to take the call."

"It will only take a minute."

The driver looks into his rearview mirror at Sarai, then turns to her. He is caught off guard seeing her staring back at him, and he feels her distain.

Sarai is sitting with her arms across her chest, and before he can utter a word she belts out of a contorted face, "What the hell is going on?" She has had enough of his shenanigans.

"I am secret service, ma'am. Your father agreed to work with the federal government and local Montgomery police concerning threats against your life and other family members from Mr. Russell Belding. I have been assigned to protect you. We will discuss the details later, with the rest of your family and supporting law enforcement. I need to get you to a safe location. Your family has been moved to a undisclosed building.

"I'm sorry for the vulgarity of my conversation, it is brash and informal, but there really is no other way for me to tell you at this point."

He reaches over the seat to hand her his cellular phone.

"Here you go. Please take the call and open your computer."

Nervously she takes the phone and grabs her laptop. Her right hand shakes as she tries to hold on to her laptop with her left hand to prevent it from falling to the floor. She can hear her laptop going off: "You've got mail."

Red Eye says, "Madam, please look at the message you just received to your e-mail. There is a code that is ten digits in length."

Sarai begins to review her e-mail. "I see it, mister driver."

"People call me Red Eye." He looks back at her again through the rear-view mirror to see her response. It is just short of repulsion. The day is not what she had expected.

"If you would punch that code into that phone, it will block any attempts at tapping that line."

Sarai does as she is told. Shaking uncontrollably, she reluctantly puts the phone to her ear and takes a deep breath.

"Hello, may I ask who is speaking?" says the voice on the other end.

"This is Miss Sarai Chameleon."

"Hello, Sarai, it is me. Secret service has assigned me the code name Dating Dot."

"You're going to have to forgive me. I'm a little confused. What is this about?" Her stomach drops and she breaks out in a sweat. "Oh my God!" Sarai has recognized the voice on the other end of the call. "What's going on? This cannot be!"

Sarai collapses onto the leather limousine seat with the phone still gripped in her hand, exhausted from the events of the day compounded by the unexpected call. She can hear the caller screaming out from the phone.

"Oh Lord, Sarai! Answer me! Sarai! I didn't plan this. It's not my fault, I can explain!"

The driver stops the car, takes the phone and interrupts the call.

"Sarai is no longer available to speak at this time."

"But—"

"I assure you she is fine. Good day."

There is a moment of silence.

"What just happened, Red Eye?"

He dials another number. "Sir, we have a major problem. Potential compromise."

"Copy that, Red Eye. Get the situation under control. Do not panic," says the voice on the other end.

Red Eye is still pulled off to the side of the highway.

"Boy!" comes from the caller. "Hear me, you better make this go away, and I mean quickly. This situation is not something that can be visible. Do whatever you can to white this out. Do you understand the command?"

Red Eye answers, "Situation concerning Sarai Chameleon and Dating Dot will be contained, sir."

"Affirmative, Mr. Red Eye."

"My shoes are special shoes for discerning feet."
Manolo Blahnik

A SNEAK PEEK INTO BOOK 2

Featuring Sarai Chameleon

by

Theresa Ward

She Wore the Name summary for Book II

After unmasking the lurid lifestyle of Sarai's only sister's husband, Russell Belding, the Chameleon sisters make a vow to recompense him for years of horror he ravaged upon both their lives.

At Nayia's deathbed, legal papers have been signed to give custody of her unborn child to Sarai. Sarai promises to take care of her sister's only seed no matter what the cost, with the cost very well being her own life.

Sarai knows that she is dealing with a dangerous and powerful man. Russell is served proof of his elicit past as well as guardianship rights that now belong to Sarai—a small price, she feels, for the evil he unleashed that caused her womb to be barren.

With revenge on his tongue, he makes his own promise to crush Sarai and the Chameleon empire, take his daughter back and raise her as the heiress to the Belding estate.

Sarai returns to Birmingham and takes refuge with her secret admirer, who has made his interest in her known. However, unbeknownst to Sarai, there are two others who desire her love, power, and attention. One of the admirers is no longer agreeable to waiting in the background and will sacrifice everything to gain Sarai's devotion.

An anonymous phone call arranged by her driver almost puts her in the grave. The driver is secret service and Sarai has no idea her life is in that much danger. The caller is known, but how will they make a play in the new life Sarai thinks she has? This person holds the trump card!

In addition, clamoring skeletons of voodoo, murder, and incest make up a deadly stew of deception and revenge sent straight from Hades, threatening to massacre two very puissant legacies.

Who will survive, and at what price?

Stay tuned!

See you on the next page of Book II

Characters:
Sarai Chameleon
Russell Belding
His lover, Tapestry Blue
Marcus, Sarai's business partner
Renee, Sarai's best friend
Jackie, the office manager
Dating Dot, in witness protection
Terrance Rutherford, Marcus's frat brother
Mr. Gary Ross, Sarai's confidant
The housekeeper, Pinky
Mr. "Catch the Red Eye," secret service
The notorious Bread Man
The diabolical Cody Rain
and . . .
Madam Matisse LaCroix, Voodoo Queen:
"No need to call me, man, I been seen you two
miles before you knocked on me door."
"Pay me now, cash only!"
"There be none of that white man shit
of credit cards to trace me!"
"Now, what spell do you need?"
MO: code name Missouri:
"Red Eye, affirmative, I got your message."
"As you know, when they go low, we go high."
"The case involving the murder of a sixteen-year-
old girl, just a gunshot away from Magnolia
Springs, Alabama, must be reopened."

"We do not care that there may be judicious evidence that leads to justifiable homicide."

"This death could cause a race war."

"By the way, I am seeing Red. I should not be seeing him! His watch ended."

"We are now in the blue, and hope to maintain that with the next election

"Call me back, Red Eye." "MO."

"My aching head. What time is it?"

Secret service agent Red Eye reaches for a bottle of pain pills from the dresser next to him, arms superbly cut and tanned a golden brown. A young man, still in his early thirties, yet the rest of his body is crumbled like an old football player who has played beyond his years as an offensive left tackle.

In addition, he has been up all night into the early morning, with little or no sleep at all. He is sometimes crammed into undercover vehicles too small for his size, giving him no leg room for circulation.

He has been chasing the criminal-minded through alleyways and tumbling on broken glass and barbed wire while getting his ass kicked by stray mad dogs and overzealous motherfuckers who have beaten the system for so long that they are willing to take the life of law enforcement.

Ring, ring! "Code blue, urgent call, pick up immediately!" The announcement comes across his phone. These type of calls must be answered on the first announcement, or it can cost you your unit as an intelligence agent. In some cases, because of the situation at hand and who is involved, as well as their level, it can cost you your life. If those behind the call are kind, you can end up in another country as a prostitute for Al-Qaeda in a hundred-and-twenty-degree weather. Life expectancy is about a month, lodged in your mind with eternal shame, never to be forgotten. Raped with brooms, poles, high-powered weapons. Forced into orgies with the drunkard leadership of Sunni Islamists.

Red Eye Leaps up.

"I'm here sir, yes sir!"

"Thank you for taking my call."

"Yes, sir!"

"Is the girl in a safe location?"

"Yes, sir."

"Good. Has she been briefed?"

"Yes sir, but there has not been much communication with Sarai Chameleon. Currently she is taking care of her sister's newborn daughter. She was told that her life is in danger because of her brother-in-law, Russell Belding, who has been taken into custody for threats against her and her family. Her parents and close affiliations have been briefed with the same information, sir."

"What close affiliates are you referring to, Red Eye?"

"Her business partner and her best friend. They happen to be married, sir. A boyfriend. They are not an immediate threat. Minimum surveillance on them, sir."

"Listen to me now."

Red Eye takes a deep breath, exhales, and urinates on his bedroom's hardwood floors. Fear turns him stark white. It takes everything in him to collect what is left of his strength. He braces the phone tightly with his right hand and his huevos with his left.

"Six of the seven have chosen to sign a deal with us. There is one more that is stalling. His signature is needed, one way or the other. If he chooses not to agree, take his right index finger. The rest of his body can be disposed of however his own will wants to dispose of it. His finger will be kept and used for access to various mega proclamations and decrees."

Red Eye exhales and the caller can hear him.

"No worries, zeen man. Me come soon, bredren. Mi deh yah. You be free soon."

Red Eye shivers with great revulsion and worry. The voice changes on the other end to another language: pat-taw and the voice of the devil.

"Those people belong to us, our establishments. Those loyalties go back to biblical honors. The body of Christ is not a secret to Satan. We own the majorities, and they will surrender to no other name. The last man is an apostle, with great influence, and we prefer to keep him alive. We also have the approval of three countries and the last one will join soon: Germany. That is just a matter of the changing of guards."

The caller pauses and moans.

"Oh, the aches and pains in my body, the longing for the taste of blood. Flu-tram, it hurts, protect me in your name, my Great Father, oh, make me young again. The youth of King David bestowed selfishly upon me, my Great Master! Red Eye, I must go now. One more thing: is it true?"

"Yes sir, I am afraid so. We think he is asleep in Russia. No awakening of movement in any other country. However, traffic analysis from some messages he sent out lately gives us a strong signal that his plans are to arrive in the United States by winter. We have the best intelligence in the world, and we cannot stop his movement yet, sir. Cody Rain is on the most wanted list of every major country. We will find out how he manages to fly under the radar, as if he actually exists. The footprints that we do have are left purposely by him and his accomplices. He is invisible to secret service, the FBI, the CIA and the KGB. However, no one can stay erased, sir."

"The update on Cody is not what I wanted to hear. I am up all night. I cannot eat, I cannot screw my wife or partner. I have aged twenty years because of this man. Do you understand me, Red Eye?"

The caller moans again from pain.

"I want him in my bed like every other leader of the world. Do you understand me, son?"

"Yes sir, Mr. President."

Advance the Read!

Here is your challenge:

Did you know that leisure reading is at an
all-time low in the United States?
The share of Americans who read for pleasure on a
given day has fallen by more than 30 percent since
2004, according to the *latest American Time Use
Survey* from the Bureau of Labor Statistics.

That is why I am inviting you to **advance the read**
by inviting others to join my reader's circle!

Reading promotes, relaxation, releases stress, and promotes
laughter while allowing you to tap into your creative side.

Let me know how you reached out to advance
the reading of *She Wore the Name.*
You can contact me through my various
outlets of social media or my website.
Help to increase my reading circle and win prizes or
scholarship to begin your own journey of writing!

I want to know!
Remember, reading can invigorate, provoke, and heal the psyche!

I want to know:
What does your name mean to you?
You are superlative, so write it out and move in your destiny!

*My name means*_____

Be the essence of the month by posting what your name
means on my website! www.sheworethename.com
I review the entries every month. You could
possibly be the winner of a prize!
Just follow the instructions.
Thank you, I appreciate you and your time!

Contact Page

Interest in plays or possible movie inquiries,
please contact Theresa A. Ward, Author at
SheWoreTheName.com
Your call will be returned within 48 hours.

-

For information on events our contest prizes,
please contact Deborah Adams at
SheWoreTheName.com

-

Press Release replies are sent via e-mail
For information on press releases, book
reviews, blogging or my podcast,
please contact Mrs. Takara Carter at
She WoreTheName.com

-

Inquiries related to
Book Trailer
YouTube video
Tok-Tok video
Facebook/Twitter/Instagram/Goodreads
Please contact Paranaka Ward at
SheWoreTheName.com

-

Inquiries related to
Humanitarian Services & Scholarships
Please contact Phyllis Clayborne at
SheWoreTheName.com

-

To purchase She Wore The Name, shop
online *at* Barnes & Noble or Amazon

ACKNOWLEDGEMENTS

I would like to thank my staff for all their hard work - Paranaka Ward, social media, videos & website Deborah Adams, event planning and prizes Takara Carter for marketing, advertising, press releases, podcasting, book discussions, as well as reviews Phyllis Clayborne, Scholrships & Humanitarian efforts Bailee Smith, creative director junior (twelve years old) Legacy Jackson, creative director junior (ten years old) Layla Jackson, motivational coach (three years old) Londyn Jackson, in charge of the ruler—everyone was on time and projects completed! (two years old)

CPSIA information can be obtained
at www.ICGtesting.com
Printed in the USA
BVHW081544201121
622107BV00002B/52